TOMORROW ALWAYS COMES

During the Second World War, Laura March left her home village of Winford to work in Scotland. But when her father became ill, she decided to return to take care of him. Laura is shocked when she comes face to face with her old love, Harry Lomax, who is accompanying a group of children being evacuated from London. Four years ago, Harry had walked out on Laura with no explanation. Now he was back, as if nothing had happened. Was her hurt still too deep to trust him again?

Books by Marlene E. McFadden
in the Linford Romance Library:

PATH OF TRUE LOVE

MARLENE E. McFADDEN

◆

TOMORROW ALWAYS COMES

Complete and Unabridged

LINFORD
Leicester

First published in Great Britain in 2003

First Linford Edition
published 2004

McFadden, Marle

British Library CIP Data

Tomorrow always
comes /
McFadden, ~~~~~~~~~ (Marlene Elizabeth), 1937 –
Tomorrow always comes.—Large print ed.—
Margaret E.
Linford ~~~~~ romance library
ROM LP
1. Love ~~~~~~~~
2. Large~~~~ type books
1568569
I. Title
823.9'14 [F]

ISBN 1–84395–211–4

Published by
F. A. Thorpe (Publishing)
Anstey, Leicestershire

Set by Words & Graphics Ltd.
Anstey, Leicestershire
Printed and bound in Great Britain by
T. J. International Ltd., Padstow, Cornwall

This book is printed on acid-free paper

1

Laura was the only passenger to alight at Winford station, almost the only person on the train at all at that stage. She stood on the platform, holding on to her suitcase, the obligatory gas mask slung around her neck on a piece of cord, and watched the train move off.

Under the railway bridge it went and into the dark tunnel, soon disappearing from view. It was close to eleven and very dark, the station building's feeble, wavering light doing little to relieve the gloom.

'Laura!'

She turned at the sound of the voice, and out of the darkness he came. As he was wearing a long black overcoat and a Homburg hat, only his face showed, a pale, smiling face, so well remembered, so beloved.

'Dad!'

Ben March took his daughter in his arms and gave her a fierce hug and a noisy kiss of welcome. His face felt cold against Laura's warm one.

Concerned for him she said, 'Have you been waiting long?'

'Not long,' but she knew he would have been at the station early.

'Come on, let's get you home,' she said, pushing her arm through his.

He was much taller than she was, and she wasn't short, but as she held on to his arm, Laura was aware that he had lost weight since she had seen him last. But then, he had been ill, pneumonia, though he had not felt inclined to let her know until three days ago, only when he believed he was well on the way to recovery. Immediately, she had arranged to come home, and refused to listen to his protestations.

He tried now to take her suitcase but she held on to it fiercely.

'It's all right,' she said, then quickly and lightly added, 'I hope you've got a fire going. I'm very cold.'

He turned to smile at her.

'Yes, I have. I'm lucky to get the wood, of course. Coal's like gold around here. They bring it for me every week, from the big house.'

'They?' Laura asked as she looked up at him.

'The Polish family, Peter, Anya and their son, Tom, oh, and Anya's nephew, Anton.'

They were walking up the hill from the station towards the manse which stood at the very top.

'How long have they been here?' Laura asked, very much aware that her father's breathing was laboured.

'Oh, only a few months, though they've been in England a lot longer than that. They fled the Nazi oppression, Laura. I don't know their story very well. If they want to tell me any details I expect they'll do it in their own time. Peter works at the mill. He's a textile engineer, a very likeable man.'

Laura smiled to herself. Her father had been minister of the Salem

3

Methodist Chapel in Winford for twenty years. Laura herself had been only three when they moved there. Ben knew everybody and everybody knew Ben. It didn't matter whether they were chapel goers or Anglicans, worshipping at St Paul's in the neighbouring village of Browdal.

It didn't matter if they never went to church or chapel, everybody he met was a friend of Ben March. But he would never push himself on to them. He would wait for them to come to him, and they did. It was typical of him that he knew so little of the Polish immigrants. When they were ready to speak about their past, they would, and Ben would be there to listen.

They had reached the house now. It was large, much too large for one man. Ben had always said there should be a family there, filling the rooms, but since Laura's mother had died the year after they came to Winford, and later Laura had moved to Scotland to work, Ben had lived alone, coping by himself, proud of his independence. Only when he became ill had he agreed to have a housekeeper, and then only on a daily basis apparently.

He had told Laura very little of his illness, but she did know he had also had a district nurse calling twice a day during the worst time. Well, she was here now and she would look after him. Mrs Walshaw was a good woman, a homely mother of six whose husband was serving with the Royal Artillery, and Laura knew her father would have been in very capable hands, but she had already written to Mrs Walshaw saying she was coming home to care for her father and she would, of course, visit her as soon as she could, the next day probably, to express her gratitude in person.

Ben had left a light burning in the hall. It was a question of darting inside as quickly as they could, so that the light, not a very strong one, wouldn't spill outside. Once the door was closed and locked for the night, however, Ben went round the living-room, switching on lamps. The black-out screens and heavy curtains were already in position. Laura was sure not even the keenest-eyed warden would be able to shout at them, 'Watch that light! Don't you know there's a war on?'

She put down her suitcase and removed her hat, shaking out her long, sleek fair hair. Ben stood in the doorway observing her keenly.

Laura hung her coat in the hall and went to hold her hands out to the warm blaze of the log fire.

'Oh, this is lovely,' she murmured.

'What was the journey like?' Ben asked.

'Not too bad, though the carriages were packed, mostly with servicemen and women, but they certainly kept the atmosphere lively.'

'Hungry?'

'No, not really. I brought plenty of sandwiches with me and a flask, but a cup of fresh tea would be nice, thank you, Dad.'

Laura would have offered to make the tea herself but she knew he wouldn't let her. She would let him take care of her for a while, cosset her, because she knew it would bring him pleasure to do so, but come tomorrow, she would put her foot down with a firm hand!

While Ben made the tea, Laura took her case upstairs to her old room. She had no need to ask if that's where she would be sleeping. The room was cold, but Laura slid her hand underneath the sheets and felt the warmth of the hot water bottle. She removed her night-dress from the case and wrapped it around the bottle.

Her suitcase wasn't particularly large. She had left most of her things at the hotel in Arrochar, but once she was settled, once her father had accepted the idea that she was here to stay, for that was certainly her intention, she was going to have her belongings sent down by train.

She had already made arrangements

for this to be done and her trunk was packed. She wouldn't tell her father yet that she had also given in her notice. He wouldn't be pleased when he finally found out, but that was just too bad. She could be as stubborn as he was!

When she went back downstairs the tea was ready, set on a small table before the fire, with a plate of ginger biscuits. Laura smiled.

'My favourites!' she cried.

'Of course. Did you think I would forget?'

Laura poured the tea. It was a cosy, homely scene. She rested her head on the back of the wing chair and closed her eyes.

'Tired, darling?' Ben asked gently.

At once she opened her eyes again.

'A little,' she admitted.

'I've had an electric fire in your room for a few hours, but I didn't dare leave it on when I went out. It's only a small thing but it burns electricity like mad, and the trouble is when it's switched off, the room soon loses its heat.

Impossible to warm these big rooms, of course. Always was, but now . . . '

Laura reached for a biscuit and munched on it happily.

'I suppose things are pretty quiet in Scotland,' Ben remarked next.

'Certainly in Arrochar, but I wouldn't say everywhere, Dad, and I was only a few miles from Glasgow, you know. I was perfectly safe, Dad, at least as safe as it'll be here. And it must be fairly safe or they wouldn't be sending the evacuees there, would they?'

Ben nodded thoughtfully, staring into the fire.

'Poor little mites. We're getting some up here.'

Neither of them spoke for several moments, each contemplating the horrors of war. Laura reached for another biscuit.

'Careful,' her father joked. 'You'll get fat.'

'Me?' Laura laughed. 'I don't think so.'

She was very slim, perhaps too much

so and it wasn't because she didn't eat. She had a very healthy appetite. She supposed she was just lucky in that respect. It was lovely sitting by the fire but Laura was becoming drowsier by the minute. She only just managed to stifle a large yawn. Smiling, Ben put down his cup and saucer.

'Come on, little one, let's get you to bed,' he said.

'You've been saying that since I was three years old,' Laura teased him.

'As long as that?' Ben said in surprise.

They both stood up and Ben put his hands on Laura's shoulders.

'It's so good to have you home, darling,' he said.

'And it's good to be home, Dad,' Laura told him.

For a moment, he pretended to look stern.

'But I don't want you mollycoddling me, do you hear?'

'As if I would!'

He kissed her cheek.

'Tomorrow I'll be down at the school helping to sort out the evacuees.'

'When are they expected?'

'Around noon, I believe.'

'A whole crowd?'

'Enough. As many as we can accommodate. We have some good people here, Laura, good people.'

And none better than Benjamin March, Laura thought.

She said good-night then and went up to her room. She undressed in seconds and was soon snuggled into the warm bed, huddled under the blankets. She listened for sounds of her father coming to bed, too, but could hear nothing. She knew he would be banking down the fire, putting up the fireguard, checking all the doors first. But Laura was fast asleep long before Ben retired for the night.

When Laura came downstairs the next morning, her father had already prepared their breakfast. The kitchen table was laid with a blue and white checked cloth. There was blue and white crockery, a dish of marmalade, toast in a rack, and a small crock of yellow butter which looked real! Ben was just removing boiled eggs from a pan and setting them in egg cups.

'Three-minute eggs, Laura, just as you like them,' Ben said to her. 'I heard you moving about so I knew when to put them in.'

'Dad, where did the eggs and butter come from?' she asked, picking up the folded, checked napkin and placing it across her knees.

Ben winked and touched the side of his nose. Laura was horrified.

'Not black market!' she cried.

'Oh, no, don't be silly. We have farmers around here, love, and lots of people keep the odd hen or two. I even contemplated putting up a hen-run myself. Plenty of room round the back, you know. Make do and mend remember,' Ben said.

Laura cracked the top of her egg. It was just as she liked it. She cut up her bread into soldiers.

'Well,' Ben remarked, sitting opposite her, 'it's a nice day for it.'

She knew he was referring to the arrival of the evacuees.

'A bit nippy earlier on but the mist's gone. A lovely, autumnal day, I expect it'll be.'

'You're waxing very lyrical this morning, Dad.'

'I feel good, that's why. I've been so frustrated lately, what with being ill, not being able to get about, feeling so helpless.'

'You do what you can. No man can do more.'

'I should have enlisted as an army chaplain,' Ben said dogmatically.

Laura stared at him.

'You're too old, Dad!'

'Too old and too unfit, go on say it,' but he was smiling at her and Laura knew he hadn't meant the remark about enlisting seriously.

He was a good minister, not just a man who stood in a pulpit twice on Sundays, baptised babies, officiated at weddings and funerals. He cared for his people, especially now at this time when the war had taken away most of the young men of the village, when new wives were left alone and there were fatherless children to feed and clothe.

Laura and her father had kept up a regular correspondence. She knew there were always functions in the school hall, lantern lectures, pea-and-pie suppers, beetle drives, married ladies' concerts. Ben had started a group at the chapel for youngsters of any age. He called it Sunshine Corner. No, Ben March had nothing to reproach himself for.

'I expect you'll feel a bit strange going to the school,' Ben remarked.

'Strange?'

'You know, seeing where Harry . . . '

Ben broke off when he saw the expression on Laura's face.

'Oh, darling, I'm sorry. That was a stupid and thoughtless thing to say.'

'It's all right, and anyway, I have other memories of Winford council school, remember. I started my education there. It doesn't just mean the place where Harry Lomax taught for a while.'

She tried to speak lightly. She knew her father hadn't meant to hurt her, but the memories she had deliberately tried to suppress, memories she knew she would have to face now she was home again, had been forced on her so much sooner than she had anticipated.

'But you are over Harry, aren't you, Laura?'

Ben was desperate, Laura knew. He had spoken out of turn, not waited till she had felt able to mention Harry's name and she knew that would have mortified him.

'Of course I am. Don't worry, Dad. It was a long time ago. I was eighteen and it was just a crush. Besides, Harry was much too old for me. Didn't you say that at the time?'

'Yes, but I only wanted your happiness, darling, you know that.'

Laura reached across the table and

patted his hand lovingly.

'I'll be able to go into the school without any qualms. You want me there, don't you, when you go to meet the evacuees?'

Ben's face brightened.

'Certainly I do. Shall we take one in?'

'Would you like to?'

This idea hadn't occurred to Laura. They had the room, that was true and her father would want to help in any way he could.

Ben smiled.

'Well, we'll see how it goes, see how many arrive. I've already had lots of offers of help. Even Mrs Walshaw's put her name down.'

Laura sighed.

'But she can't possibly have the room, not with six of her own.'

'Dear Mrs Walshaw's heart is big enough to love another child, and she'll make certain her home is big enough, too, if necessary.'

Harry's name was not mentioned again and soon after breakfast Ben retired to his study to commence work on his next Sunday's sermon, leaving Laura to wash up and make the beds. Ben had already cleared out the ashes in the grate and laid the new logs and kindling. They wouldn't put a match to the fire till much later in the day.

But Harry Lomax was now very much on Laura's mind. She hadn't told her father the truth. She hadn't got over Harry. She didn't think she ever would. She had had offers of dates from male guests at the hotel over the past four years and from some of the locals. She had even accepted a few of those invitations, but never more than once with the same man. What she had felt for Harry Lomax, nine years her senior, had most definitely not been a crush. She had loved him very much and he had professed to love her.

They had met at a social evening at the school in 1935. Harry had only recently joined the staff there, having come up from London, to live, as he frequently teased Laura, in the sticks.

He taught English. He was tall, good looking and laughed a lot. He also, to Laura's surprise, as she had met so few men who did, turned out to be an excellent dancer.

After that first meeting, Laura and Harry had seldom been apart. At first, Ben had disapproved of their relationship, not in any heavy-handed way. Ben would never have been like that. He had genuinely liked Harry, found him courteous and well-educated and because of that liking, he had accepted Harry as a frequent visitor at the manse. Laura knew her father was aware how she and Harry felt about one another, and the only mild criticism he made was to say he thought Laura was too young for a serious relationship and that there was too large a gap in their ages.

However, once he knew how deeply they were in love he had been pleased for Laura. There had been no official engagement but they had certainly talked about marriage. Then, one day, without any warning, Harry was gone. True, he left her a letter, giving what he must assume was a valid explanation, but nothing made sense to a devastated Laura. The school governors were equally shocked and surprised when one of their favourite teachers left without any real notice. Laura had no way of contacting Harry and he never tried to contact her.

It took a long, long time for Laura to be able to continue with her life. Then she enrolled in a secretarial college, learned shorthand and typing quickly and efficiently and took herself off to a job as a live-in receptionist at a hotel in Scotland. If Ben March was unhappy to see his beloved daughter leave home, he tried to hide it. He gave her his blessing, knowing the move was important to Laura, to both her well-being and future happiness.

The name of Harry Lomax had not been mentioned by either of them from that day onwards, until now, that is, and that morning, as she kept busy doing totally unnecessary housework Laura began to believe her father's mention of Harry was the best thing that could have happened. It had been said now, and there would be no awkward moments between them where Laura could possibly be waiting for her father to say something and he could have been worrying unnecessarily that he might inadvertently put his foot in it.

Harry would be in Laura's mind in a vivid way for some time, she supposed. There were times, of course, when she never gave him a thought. There were others, equally, when she lay awake at nights remembering him with an aching longing, but this present ache would fade, as it always had before. She was here to start a new life now. Great Britain was at war. There was a great deal for her to do, many ways in which she could help.

When Laura and Ben arrived at the school later that morning, the hall was buzzing with anticipation. Most of the village people were there. Laura knew most of them, of course, and went around talking to them. There was Frank Draper and his wife, Annie, who ran the local fish-and-chip shop; George Farrand, the butcher from the co-operative store; Miss Cook who had a sweet shop and was a great favourite with the local children. She had never married, so had no children of her own but she was still a sprightly, energetic woman, with a perpetual twinkle in her eye and generally a toffee or two in her pocket. Laura wondered how Miss Cook was coping now that sweets and confectionery were rationed.

She soon noticed Mrs Walshaw and went across to her.

'Laura, lass,' Mrs Walshaw greeted her.

'Hello, Mrs Walshaw,' Laura said. 'I want to thank you for looking after Dad so well.'

Mrs Walshaw laughed.

'Think nowt of it, lass,' she said. 'It was a pleasure. Your dad's a proper gentleman. No trouble at all.'

She glanced across the hall to where Ben was chatting to the school's headmaster.

'He made a wonderful recovery, didn't he? Tough as old boots he is.'

'The children should be here soon,' Laura remarked.

'Aye. I'll probably take in a bairn myself.'

'Are you sure you'll be able to manage?' Laura asked.

'What, me? 'Course I will. I'll double up my Jimmy and Brian if it's a boy and our Marlene and Dorothy if it's a girl. No trouble at all.'

And Laura was sure it wouldn't be, not for the wonderful Mrs Walshaw.

'My eldest two work now, you know. Yes, our Derek's been taken on at the co-op, in the butchery department. And our Lawrence got married last year, so there's only the five at home now. Our Lawrence could be called up any time now. To me he's still a bairn, but with there being a war and all . . . '

She shook her head sadly.

'Anyway, as I was saying, I've always got the room.'

'I didn't know your son had married,' Laura said.

'Aye. She's a grand lass. I've gained a daughter, as they say, another daughter. My others, they were a bit put out not to be here this morning but Mr Hiram insisted the school morning shouldn't be disturbed, so they're all in their classes.'

Ben appeared at Laura's shoulder with news of the bus's arrival.

'It's pulled into the yard,' he said. 'Good morning, Mrs Walshaw.'

'Good morning to you.'

'It's my understanding, from what Mr Hiram was telling me, that there are only twenty children coming to Winford so that's not too bad, is it?' he said cheerfully. 'They're all from the East End of London.'

He made their excuses and led Laura away. She was starting to feel rather excited, and nervous, too, of course. It would be a challenge taking in twenty little Cockneys, but if at all possible she really would like them to take a child at the manse. It would only be fair, and besides, she genuinely wanted to, and she was sure her father would feel the same way.

Mr Hiram had gone outside to welcome the new arrivals and a general hush had fallen on the assembled gathering. People were sitting around the edge of the hall. Laura wondered what the procedure would be. Her heart went out to those children, torn from their families, sent on a long journey by train, then bus from the nearest town, four miles away. They would be tired, scared, hungry probably, having no idea what was going to happen to them.

There were voices approaching the hall now and images appearing on the other side of the closed, half-glassed doors. Mr Hiram entered first, smiling a broad smile of welcome and encouragement.

'Come in, come in, boys and girls,' he cried.

He stood to one side, holding out his arms in a universal sign of welcome and friendship. No-one in the hall moved, or spoke, as the small band of forlorn-looking children shuffled into view. To Laura some appeared as young as four or five with the eldest being, she supposed, at least fourteen or fifteen. There seemed to be a good mixture of both sexes. Each had a label attached to their jacket or coat, and a gas mask in a cardboard box around their necks. Some clutched little bundles of belongings, some had battered suitcases. One or two of the youngest were crying.

Laura felt a huge lump forming in her throat and tears came to her eyes. She wanted to get up and run to them and put her arms around each one of them. Then she saw the last person, the person in charge, entering the hall, closing the doors quietly behind him. He was a tall man in a dark overcoat and a grey trilby hat.

As he turned from the doors and put

his hands on the shoulders of the nearest child, a boy of about twelve, Laura recognised him with such a lurch of her insides that she felt she was going to pass out. It was Harry!

2

He didn't see her at first. As everything inside her slowly subsided into its normal place, Laura heard her father saying, 'Oh, my God'. It was the first time she had ever heard him taking the Lord's name in vain and she knew that he had recognised Harry as well.

It seemed in the next few moments, as Harry removed his hat, that nearly everyone began to murmur, to exclaim. Harry looked slightly embarrassed. Laura could only stare at him, unable to avert her eyes, waiting for him to look across to where she and Ben were standing.

He hadn't changed much; still the same overly-long curly brown hair, still those same dark eyes, and the smile, for Harry was soon smiling at everyone, and waving his hand. Mr Hiram stepped forward. He, too, held up his hands, to stop the mounting chorus of remarks.

'Yes, yes, friends, it's our Harry back in Winford again. I didn't say anything to anybody because I wasn't sure until today that it would be Harry who accompanied the children, but as you can see, here he is. I'm sure you'll all be pleased to hear that he is going to teach here again, at least for the foreseeable future.'

Someone started clapping and soon everyone had joined in, everyone except Laura and Ben that is. She felt her father slip his arm around her shoulders and give them a gentle squeeze, but he didn't speak.

Harry moved nearer the centre of the hall and it was then that Laura noticed he was leaning on a stick and that he had a very pronounced limp in his right leg. He had been hurt! When? How? She moved her eyes back to his face. He was looking right at her. He nodded briefly, his expression giving nothing away, but her heart was thumping madly.

She was glad when Mr Hiram took charge again, getting back to the matter in hand — the billeting of the evacuees who were standing silent, watchful, with a mixture of expressions. Some looked even more frightened than before, some were grinning, looking up at Harry, giving Laura the impression that they knew him and liked him.

Harry made no attempt to approach her and for that she was grateful. She wouldn't have known what to say to him, not just then — perhaps later when she had got over the shock of seeing him again. Her father had moved off to speak to Mr Hiram and as Harry was standing right next to the head-master by then, Ben took Harry's hand and spoke to him, too. Harry smiled. Ben smiled. No reproaches there then, Laura thought wryly. Just like two old friends meeting after a long absence. Could she be the same? Could she go to Harry now and shake his hand and make general enquiries about his health and well-being? She didn't think she could.

She retired to the very end of the hall, sitting down again, trying not to watch Harry. The children were being urged to break into smaller groups. Adults were coming forward, some attempting to read the name labels.

Miss Cook was having none of that. She had taken the hand of a girl of about eight, led her to the side of the hall and sat with the little girl on her lap, producing the inevitable sweetie. The child stared at her with large eyes, eyes that were wary, but she took the proferred gift, unwrapped it and, encouraged by Miss Cook, popped it in her mouth. As she chewed and tasted its sweetness her face broke into a wide smile. Miss Cook looked delighted and hugged the little girl to her. She didn't protest.

And so it went on. Children were being paired off with foster parents. Laura watched them. Some were taking more than one child. Laura had not the slightest doubt that every child would find a decent, loving home. Most of the children soon appeared to be spoken for. Some people, Laura knew, would be doomed to disappointment, as there were fewer children than had been anticipated. She saw then that Harry was looking at her again and when he made a move towards her, leaning heavily on his cane, she got up abruptly and walked briskly to the other end of the hall. She wasn't ready for a confrontation.

She saw a girl sitting by herself, her legs outstretched, her head bending forward, short straight, mousey-coloured hair falling over her face. Laura went and sat beside her.

'Hello,' she said. 'I'm Laura. What's your name?'

The girl looked up. She was at least fourteen and Laura couldn't help noticing that she was very well developed for her age. Her crumpled grey cardigan was tight across her chest with the bottom two buttons missing.

Underneath she wore a frock with a pattern of roses, and a white Peter Pan collar, much too thin for the time of the year. Her face was narrow, but she was a bonny girl with lovely grey eyes and incredibly long lashes.

When she spoke it was with an edge of contempt.

'You can read, can't you?' she said and jerked her hand towards the label pinned to her cardigan.

Laura did as she was bid.

'Shirley. Shirley Dobson. Well, hello, Shirley.'

She held out her hand. The girl stared at it then up at Laura as though she thought Laura had gone mad.

'Wot do you want to shake 'ands for?' she enquired in a hostile voice.

'I really have no idea. Silly, isn't it? Well, Shirley, why are you sitting here by yourself?' Laura said with a smile.

' 'Cos I don't want nobody prodding and poking at me, that's why?'

'Nobody's going to do that, Shirley.'

The girl shrugged her shoulders.

'Might as well.'

She gazed around her with seeming indifference, but Laura's keen eyes noted that her mouth was trembling uncertainly.

'Would you like to come home with me?' Laura asked.

'And who are you when you're at 'ome?'

'I've told you, my name is Laura, Laura March. My father is a minister at the local chapel.'

'Not blooming likely,' Shirley cried. 'I'm not going to no Sunday school!'

'You don't have to go to Sunday School if you don't want to,' Laura assured her.

'Oh, no? Pull the other leg, it's got bells on it,' Shirley sneered.

Laura had an urgent need to laugh but she daren't. That would only antagonise the girl even more. She didn't quite know how to handle the situation. Then she heard Harry's voice and he was suddenly there.

'All right, Shirley?' he enquired.

'Getting to know Laura, are you?'

Despite her wariness of Harry she had to admit that if anyone could get through to this hostile child, he was the person to do it, or her father, of course, but he was still engaged in the last-minute negotiations.

'Can I come and live wiv you, 'Arry?' Shirley asked plaintively.

'I'm afraid not, Shirley, love. You see, I'm an evacuee as well, in a way, and I'm being billeted with Mr Hiram. Now you wouldn't want to have to live with a headmaster, would you, love?'

Shirley's eyes widened in horror.

'No, I wouldn't,' she cried.

'So how about giving Laura here a chance, eh? There's a good girl. She's one of the best, is Laura, and her old man as well. They live in a big house. You'd have your own room, wouldn't have to share with nobody.'

'Honest?'

'Cross my heart and hope to die,' Harry said solemnly.

Shirley stood up.

'All right,' she said resolutely. 'I'll give it a go.'

Harry shot Laura a glance. In that instant, her heart warmed to him. She couldn't help it. Could they let bygones by bygones, start all over again? She pulled herself up sharply. Harry was here to do a job, to teach and to help care for these children. She mustn't forget that.

'Come on, then, Shirley,' she said. 'I expect you're starving hungry.'

'Sure am,' Shirley declared.

Unexpectedly, she gave Laura a friendly grin and Laura, thanking Harry silently, believed the first battle had been won. They turned away from him, but Harry caught hold of Laura's arm.

'Laura,' he whispered urgently, 'I've got to talk to you. Oh, not now, when it's convenient. This evening?'

Laura hesitated, very aware of the pressure of his fingers on her arm.

'Harry, I . . . ' she began.

'Please,' he emphasised.

Laura gave in.

'All right. What time? Where?'

'In the station buffet at eight. Will that be all right?'

'I'll be there,' she said and turned away from him again.

Perhaps she was a fool, but she had to meet him. Perhaps he would be able to shed some light on the real reason he went away so abruptly. She wouldn't delude herself into believing there might be some hope for them, but talking couldn't hurt, could it?

★　★　★

She was a good few minutes early for her meeting with Harry. There was no-one else in the small, dingy room, just a woman behind the counter, not someone Laura knew, though she had been pleasant enough. Whilst she waited, nursing a cup of tea, the station porter strolled in, going to the counter, leaning on it casually, smoking a cigarette. Laura didn't know him either though he nodded politely in her direction. He and the woman started up a conversation, grousing in general about this and that and the other.

Laura sat waiting patiently for Harry. She didn't want to be away from the house too long, not on Shirley's first night. The girl had had a bath and she'd left her sitting drinking a mug of cocoa, wearing Laura's old dressing-gown, talking quite happily to Ben.

'Can I stay up till you get back, Laura?' she had pleaded.

Laura hesitated for only a second. She couldn't resist the appeal in Shirley's lovely eyes.

'All right,' she said. 'I won't be late.'

Handling Shirley had been far easier than she had anticipated. Her initial hostility seemed to have vanished and she was proving to be a chatty, bright youngster. When Laura took her back to the manse she had looked around her in amazement at the size of the place. Ben hadn't yet returned from the school, though he had been introduced to Shirley.

'Blimey,' Shirley cried, 'is there only the two of you living 'ere?'

'Just the two of us,' Laura replied.

Shirley went from room to room, flinging open doors, growing more excited with every room she saw. Laura had already decided which room Shirley should have, not too big and not too small. She wished they had had more time so they could perhaps have re-painted the room, hung up some pretty new curtains, but consoled herself with the fact that materials might have been hard to come by. The three-quarter size bed was covered with a pale green eiderdown and only needed bedding. There was a dressing-table, a small wardrobe and a green-painted chair with a pink cushion. There was also a nice view of the rear garden which backed on to a steep, rocky bank.

Shirley turned to Laura in disbelief. 'This is to be my room?' she asked.

'Yes.' Laura smiled.

'All on me own?'

'Of course.'

Shirley went and bounced on the bed.

'It's so big! I sleep on a camp bed at 'ome and me bruvvers share the room. Three of 'em. You have brothers?' Laura asked. 'Are they here as well?'

She hated the idea that Shirley would be separated from her siblings, but didn't think she and her father could cope with three more children, who, anyway, would obviously have gone to other foster homes by now.

'Oh, no,' Shirley said. 'They've gone to me auntie in Devon. Lives on a farm she does and she says the lads can be a big 'elp to her. Unpaid servants, more likely. Didn't want me, on account of me being a girl.'

'Oh, I see,' Laura said.

'Anyway,' Shirley went on with a cheeky grin, 'I'd rather be 'ere where I can have me own room.'

She talked non-stop. It was a pleasure

to see her excitement but when she saw the last room of all, the huge bathroom, words failed her.

When she did find her voice again it was to say, 'A proper barf, wiv taps and an inside lavvy. Ooh, can I 'ave a barf? Can I? Please!'

Laura smiled.

'Well, I'll have to light the fire first and get the water heated, later, certainly before you go to bed. Now, what about your clothes, Shirley?'

Shirley's face fell. Laura had noticed the girl only had a rough bundle which was obviously a home-made travelling bag.

'Haven't got much,' the girl mumbled, holding aloft the pathetic bag.

'Let's have a look then.'

Laura tried to sound cheerful and encouraging as Shirley put the bag on the bed. She up-ended the bag and shook its contents on to the eiderdown. Laura counted two pairs of grubby socks, two pairs of navy blue knickers, a much-darned vest, a fleecy liberty bodice, a navy blue skirt, a ghastly striped jumper, a small black comb and a small bundle wrapped in a piece of flannel. Shirley was watching her closely.

'That's only me soap and stuff and things.'

'I've got some clothes in my wardrobe,' Laura began, 'things I've grown out of and you're not so much smaller than I am, are you?'

She went and stood close to Shirley to emphasise her words.

'Would you like to look at them?'

'Well, me ma don't like us to accept charity,' she said.

'It wouldn't be charity. You'd be doing me a favour. I can hardly close my wardrobe door.'

Shirley beamed.

'Oh, well, in that case, I suppose it'll be all right.'

The vision of Shirley's happiness and excitement when she was allowed to chose which items she wanted came back to Laura as she waited for Harry.

She glanced at the buffet clock. He was a good five minutes late, but Laura didn't mind. He probably had a good reason to be late.

She decided to give him till at least quarter past. Perhaps he wouldn't come at all. Her mind went back to earlier in the day when her father had come home. Shirley had become shy when she saw him, standing close to Laura, biting her nails, but her shyness hadn't lasted long.

'Now what shall we eat?' Laura said.

'I've got half of one of George Farrand's pork pies in the larder,' Ben said, 'and some pickles, a bit of cheese and some nice crusty bread. What do you say, Shirley?'

'Ooh, ta,' were Shirley's only words.

She looked neat and trim in Laura's brown gored skirt and apple green fluffy jumper. Ben cocked his eyebrow at her.

'Now, who's this smart young lady?' he said in a gentle, teasing voice.

To Laura's delight, Shirley giggled with pleasure.

42

Laura could see by her father's expression that he wanted to have an urgent word with her and she could guess what it would be about. She suggested to Shirley that she go and sit in the living-room till lunch.

'Read my books if you want,' she said, hoping her Enid Blytons were still on the bookshelf and being sure they would be. 'I've got Ludo and Snakes and Ladders as well,' she added.

Shirley pulled a face at that, but she went and selected a book and sat on the couch to read it. Laura realised she wouldn't have to think of Shirley as a baby. She was fourteen, in some ways already growing into a young woman. She looked back from the doorway. Shirley seemed engrossed in her choice of book.

She went into the kitchen where Ben was heating the kettle.

'Laura,' he said as he turned to her, 'are you all right?'

'Because of Harry, you mean? Yes, I'm fine. Isn't Shirley a lovely girl?'

'She certainly is. Wearing your clothes, I presume?'

Laura nodded, but Ben was not distracted from talking about Harry.

'I had no idea he was coming here, you know.'

'I know,' Laura answered as she got the tablecloth out of a drawer.

'Did you get an opportunity to speak to him?'

'Yes, and I'm meeting him later, in the station buffet.'

'Oh, love, is that wise?'

'Dad, we're going to run into one another nearly every day, aren't we? What's the point of trying to hide away? I'll have to take Shirley to school, for one thing, that is if she still goes to school. I haven't asked her yet.'

'We can take care of those sort of matters as they arise, Laura,' Ben said, 'and if you're sure you're all right about Harry . . .'

'I'm sure,' Laura said firmly.

But she wasn't, and now, as she waited, she was becoming increasingly less sure that even this arranged meeting was a good idea. What on earth would they find to say to one another? She was just beginning to hope that perhaps Harry had stood her up when the door opened and in he came.

He was carrying a torch, as she had been, which he now slipped into his overcoat pocket, supporting himself on his walking stick. He removed his hat and ran a hand through his hair. He smiled at her as he crossed to where she was sitting, taking the chair opposite her.

Laura wanted to ask him how he came to hurt his leg, but not just at that moment. She was surprised when Harry reached across the table and took hold of her hand.

'Laura,' he said in a low voice, 'I'm so sorry I'm late. It's been one heck of a day. I thought you might have gone.'

'I wouldn't do that, Harry,' Laura said, though she had been toying with the idea.

'Shall I get you more tea?'

'No, thanks.'

'Well, I suppose I'd better have some.'

He glanced at the counter.

'I think I'll risk a rock bun as well.'

He crossed to make a polite request of the woman. Laura watched him. As he waited, he half-turned towards her, undoing the buttons of his coat. He smiled again. She felt strong emotions stirring in her. She couldn't help it. Oh, dear, she was far from being the calm and controlled person she had told her father she was. She still loved Harry Lomax! Distance and years hadn't been able to destroy that love. And now that they were face to face again, well, what hope was there for her?

'I'll bring your tea,' the woman said to Harry, and he thanked her as he returned to the table.

Once more, he eased himself into a comfortable position on the chair.

'How's Shirley?' he asked.

'She's all right. Seems to be settling in well. Quite a little chatterbox.'

'That sounds like Shirley,' he said with a grin.

'How old is she, Harry?' Laura asked.

'Fourteen,' he replied.

'Is she still attending school?'

'Till next Easter. Why, has she told you she no longer goes to school?'

'No, no. I just wondered.'

'She's a nice girl. Very bright, which isn't something you can say for some of them. Comes from a nice family, a good family. They're poor, of course, but clean and honest.'

The tea and rock bun arrived. As Harry stirred his tea in thoughtful silence, Laura couldn't seem to take her eyes off him. As he bent his head, her gaze seemed to be focused on his hair. She remembered running her fingers through it, coarse and thick.

'How did you come to be involved with bringing the children up here?' she asked quickly, breaking her gaze.

'Well, I'm a teacher, aren't I, and my school, incidentally Shirley's school, needed a volunteer. Children are being sent all over the country and as there was just a small group coming here, I said I could manage them by myself, apart from a Mrs Rufford, a retired nurse, who came as far as Bletchfield with me.'

'Do you think you'll be happy staying with the Hirams?'

'It's temporary. I'm going to try to rent a place of my own before long.'

Harry bit into the rock bun. When his mouth was empty he spoke quietly.

'You need strong teeth for this.'

'That's why it's called a rock bun,' she said, smiling.

Harry replaced the rest of the bun on his plate and pushed it aside. Once more his hand slid across the table, and rested on Laura's own.

'Laura,' he began, 'why are we making small talk?'

Laura looked away from him.

'Perhaps its too dangerous to do anything else,' she said.

'Dangerous for us? But surely we've got so much to say to one another.'

'What have we to say, Harry? What is there to say? You left me and now you're back in Winford. Did you think about me when you found out you were coming here?'

'I've never stopped thinking about you, Laura.'

Laura laughed harshly.

'I very nearly wasn't here at all. I only came back last night, because my father has been ill.'

Harry looked surprised.

'Back from where?'

'Scotland. I work in a hotel there.'

She wasn't going to tell him she had given up her job.

'I didn't know that,' Harry said softly.

'There's a great deal you don't know about me, Harry.'

'Laura, I know I hurt you, but I didn't have any choice.'

The words started to flow from her then, as though she had only been waiting for the opportunity to let fly at him.

'You left me a letter. Oh, it was full of

apologies but very little else. Called away, you said. Unavoidable, you said. Was someone in your family sick perhaps? Had someone died?'

'Nothing like that,' Harry said, shaking his head.

'Then what was the true reason, Harry?'

He looked straight into her eyes.

'I'm afraid I can't tell you that.'

'Can't or won't?'

Laura was aware her voice was rising. She heard a train coming into the station and, after the banging of doors, there were footsteps and chattering voices and the buffet doors burst open as a small crowd entered. They started to place orders for food and drinks.

Laura stood up abruptly.

'Let's get out of here,' she said.

Harry got up, too.

'Don't go, Laura, please,' he begged.

'Can't we take a walk? I know it's pitch black but I've got a torch and so have you. One little beam isn't going to cause a breach of security, is it?'

'All right,' Harry said.

As it happened, it wasn't so dark. There was a moon that night, with few clouds gliding across it. As they started up the hill from the station, Laura felt a pang of guilt.

'I'm sorry, perhaps you don't want to walk.'

'I don't mind,' Harry said. 'Exercise is good for me, in moderation.'

'What happened to your leg?'

She was starting to feel calmer now.

'A car accident.'

'Recently?'

'A couple of years ago actually.'

'So your limp is a permanent one then?'

Harry smiled.

'Looks that way. Kept me out of the Forces, of course.'

'Would you have enlisted?'

'Oh, I would have joined the Air Force, no doubt about that,' Harry said.

Laura stared at him.

'Can you fly a plane?'

'As a matter of fact, I can.'

She was astounded. Harry a pilot? Was that activity abruptly cut short for ever once he was hurt? She didn't ask the question.

They were approaching the manse now. Laura hesitated by the gate. Perhaps she could take Harry inside. She really ought to go in and supervise Shirley's bedtime, but she didn't want to share Harry with her father, not just then. Without saying anything, she kept on walking, her hands in her coat pockets, and Harry didn't say anything either.

'Let's walk up past the big house,' Laura suggested.

Winford was quite a hilly village. The main road into neighbouring Bletchfield ran along the bottom of Station Lane where the manse was situated. At the top of Station Lane was a right turn into Beech Road or left to climb yet another hill. Laura and Harry took the left turn.

Terraced houses were built on the right hand side of Turner Hill Road. A wooded plantation began where the terrace of houses finished and within this plantation stood the big house. It had always simply been called that. Built by the owners of the woollen mill in Browdale, the house had at one time fallen into disrepair, but Ben had told Laura it was now occupied by the Polish family. It loomed now through the trees, large, solid-looking. From the road it was impossible to tell that the house was occupied.

'We used to play in that plantation when we were little,' Laura said. 'Of course it was private land but we didn't pay any heed to that. Some of the trees were particularly good for climbing.'

'Does anyone live there now?' Harry asked.

'According to my father there is a family of Polish immigrants there. I believe he said the husband works at the mill. I haven't seen any of them yet. Dad says they're quiet people, keeping themselves to themselves.'

'Uprooted from their homeland,'

Harry remarked, 'like so many others.'

Laura said nothing, and when Harry took hold of her hand she did not object. She was wearing gloves so couldn't feel the warmth of his fingers, but it felt nice, somehow comforting in the darkness, like they used to be, could never be again, she realised. Abruptly, she pulled free of him.

Harry said nothing for a few moments. Then he asked, 'Will you ever be able to forgive me, Laura?'

'I don't know,' she said. 'Forgive is perhaps too strong a word.'

'I want us to be friends again, during the time I'm in Winford.'

Some of her previous anger flared again at that.

'And how long will that be?' she demanded.

'Who can tell? I should imagine for the duration of the war at least.'

'Then you'll leave again, I suppose,' she flung at him.

He stopped walking and grabbed her shoulders.

'I can make no promises, Laura. No-one can, not in these times, but I want you to know that I love you, that I have always loved you, that I will always love you. There's never been anybody else. I want you to trust me, to give me a chance.'

Trust him? At one time she would have trusted him with her life. Now the hurt was still too deep. She was afraid that if she gave her love to him he would shatter it as he had before. Harry had not given her any real explanation as to why he left in the way he had, not at the time, certainly not tonight as they sat in the dingy station buffet. He wanted her to trust him blindly with no reassurances, but she didn't think she could do that.

Suddenly he was kissing her, hard and long, holding her shoulders tightly so she couldn't struggle free. After a few moments she didn't want to be free. She heard his stick clatter to the ground as his arms came about her waist and hers around his neck. When they eased away from each other, however, Laura was horrified that they had kissed like that in a public place, even though it was so dark and there wasn't a soul around to see them.

But more than that she was horrified by her own reaction.

'No, Harry, no!' she cried and left him there, standing alone, perplexed, as she ran back down the hill towards home.

By the time she reached the manse, she was out of breath. The door wasn't locked. It never was till Ben went to bed. Laura went into the hall. There was no light burning there tonight, but there was a sliver of light beneath the living-room door and she could hear the muffled tones of some wireless programme. She hung her coat in the hall and paused a few moments to compose herself and regain her breath.

Ben was sitting in his favourite armchair, a book open on his knee. Shirley was fast asleep on the couch, curled on her side, the dressing-gown tucked around her legs. Music was coming from the wireless.

'Hello, there,' Ben said with a smile. 'Isn't Harry coming in?'

'Not tonight,' Laura told him, hoping he wouldn't probe too deeply.

She didn't think he would. He would sense she didn't want to talk about Harry and that would be enough for him. Laura stared down at the slumbering Shirley.

'How long has she been asleep?'

'Not long. She tried to keep awake, but in the end she had to give in. She must have been exhausted from all the travelling.'

'Yes, I shouldn't have gone out tonight. It was thoughtless of me.'

'Oh, Shirley was all right with me, darling,' Ben said, smiling, laying aside his book. 'We played Ludo. She won, of course.'

So Shirley wasn't too old for board games after all. Laura crossed to Ben and kissed the top of his head.

'I suppose I'd better wake her and

get her to bed,' she said.

'It seems a shame to disturb her, but, yes, I suppose you'd better.'

Laura shook Shirley's shoulder gently. Immediately the girl was awake, sitting up, rubbing her eyes. Laura had expected to have to coax her awake.

'Is it morning?' Shirley asked.

'No, you've fallen asleep on the couch. Come on, up to bed you go.'

As Shirley stood up, the dressing-gown fell open, revealing the fact that she was only wearing her under-wear. Well, that meant another search through her own outgrown clothes, Laura thought, wishing she could go out and kit Shirley out in brand new clothing from head to toe. The girl clutched the gown around her, holding it tightly together.

'I think I'll have an early night, Dad,' Laura said

'As you like, dear. I shan't be too far behind you.'

'Good-night then, Dad,' she said and kissed her father once more.

58

'Good-night and God bless,' Ben returned.

'Nightie, night,' Shirley said chirpily.

As soon as Shirley was snuggled down in the warm bed she was off to sleep with the same speed with which she had just woken up. Laura tucked the covers round her, looking down at her, listening to her deep, even breathing. Perhaps she was used to being disturbed. Perhaps her family had spent nights in the air raid shelter, having to leave their beds in the middle of the night.

Laura had not experienced that herself, at least not yet, but she remembered her father writing to tell her that here in Winford, air raid sirens were not unknown. Many homes had Anderson shelters in their back gardens, but the manse would rely on its cellars.

'Good-night, Shirley,' Laura said softly and went to her own room.

For her, sleep would not come easily. She regretted running away from Harry as she had done. It was such a childish thing to do. Tomorrow she would probably see him when she enrolled Shirley at the senior school, though, as it would be Thursday, she had decided she needn't actually go to school till the following Monday, give her time to settle in first and get to know them, though she seemed perfectly at ease with them as it was.

At last, Laura did sleep but was awakened some time later by the sound of loud sobbing. At first she was disorientated, until she realised it was Shirley. She got out of bed and even though it was cold she didn't bother reaching for her dressing-gown. As she walked across the landing to Shirley's room, Ben's door opened and he put a tousled head round it.

'It's all right, Dad,' Laura said. 'I'll see to her.'

Ben didn't speak and went back to bed.

Shirley was sitting up in bed, her hands covering her face, her shoulders shaking with the intensity of her sobs. Laura went and sat on the bed and gathered the girl into her arms, smoothing a hand over her hair.

'It's all right, Shirley, it's all right. You were just having a nightmare.'

'No, I wasn't. I'd woken up and I was thinking about Ma and me brothers. I wanna go 'ome. I wanna go 'ome,' she wailed.

Laura rocked her gently. Her body was slight and she was shivering.

'You can't, love. I'm sorry, but you can't, not just yet. You've been sent up here to keep you safe from the bombs.'

Shirley looked up at her, her face wet with tears.

'What about Ma? Why can't she come 'ere 'n' all?'

'It wouldn't be possible for everybody to be evacuated, Shirley, but the Government thinks it's best for as many children as possible to be away from London.'

'How long for?' Shirley asked.

'I don't know,' was all Laura could say.

'Till Hitler stops dropping his bombs, eh?' Shirley said, calmer now.

'I suppose so.'

Shirley sniffed and settled back on to the bed. Once more, Laura tucked the covers round her. This time she bent forward and kissed Shirley's cheek.

'We'll look after you, my dad and I, and you'll make lots of new friends, go to a new school.'

Seeing the horrified look on Shirley's face, Laura wished she hadn't made that last remark.

'I know you're scared by all the changes, Shirley,' she rushed on, 'but it's a big adventure really, in a way,' she added lamely.

Shirley seemed satisfied. She even managed a small smile.

'Sorry I woke you up, Laura,' she apologised.

'That's all right. Any time.'

She went back to her own room, feeling humbled. There she was, worrying about herself, thinking her relationship with Harry was the most important thing in the world, when compared to Shirley's problems, it was nothing. She settled down in bed again and this time she was soon asleep.

3

During breakfast on Saturday morning, Ben said to Shirley, 'I'm going into town this morning, Shirley. Would you like to come with me?'

Shirley looked amazed.

'You're going up to London?' she asked.

Ben laughed.

'No, our town, Bletchfield. I shall be travelling by trolley bus. I think you'd enjoy that.'

'Ooh, yes, please.'

Laura knew that Shirley and her father were really hitting it off together, which didn't surprise her at all. So far there had been no repeat of Shirley's homesickness and she seemed to be looking forward to starting school.

As she had planned, Laura had gone to the school on the Thursday morning, taking Shirley with her, at that point, it must be said, a rather subdued Shirley. But once she saw that most of the other evacuees were there as well, once she had met the teacher who would be in charge of her class, seen her desk, got acquainted with her surroundings, Shirley seemed quite keen about it all.

Harry was there, too, of course. He had already taken up his new duties in the school. He and Laura had little time to talk, certainly not enough to do more than chat casually about Shirley and schoolwork in general. Since that morning, Laura had not seen Harry again.

After Ben and Shirley had left to catch the trolley bus at the end of Beech Road, Shirley wearing her latest acquisition, Laura's discarded green winter coat and matching beret. Laura washed the breakfast dishes, ran her father's ancient carpet sweeper over the floors and made the beds. She intended going down to the co-operative store some time that day, to do some grocery shopping.

She was sitting at the kitchen table, chewing on a pencil and trying to compile a shopping list, when she saw someone passing the kitchen window and a moment later there was a loud knocking on the door. It was unusual for anyone but trades people to come to the back door but Laura had a premonition it would be Harry. She got up from the table, her heart starting to thump and opened the door, wondering what she would find to say to him, or indeed, what he would say to her.

But it wasn't Harry. It was a man of about Harry's height and build, though somewhat younger than he was. He had swept-back dark hair and pronounced cheekbones. His eyes were deep-set and rather penetrating. He was casually dressed in brown trousers and a short brown jacket, over a checked shirt, which was open at the neck. He wasn't wearing a hat.

'Good-morning,' he began. 'Is Mr March at home, please?'

As soon as he spoke, Laura knew by

his accent that he was one of the Polish people from the big house.

'I'm sorry, he isn't,' she said.

He looked hesitant, shuffling his feet.

'May I help?' Laura asked.

'Perhaps you can. I have brought the wood, for the fire. I should have come yesterday but I could not make it.'

Laura smiled, holding out her hand.

'I'm Laura, Ben's daughter.'

He paused before shaking her hand.

'Tom Bronowski,' he said. 'I did not know Mr March had a daughter.'

'I'm here to stay for a while.'

Laura didn't think any further explanation was necessary.

'Do you want to come inside?'

She opened the door wider.

'First I will deliver the wood,' Tom said, 'and when that is finished I will come inside for the payment. Is that all right?'

'Of course.'

Ben had already told her where he kept the money to pay for the wood. The young man smiled and his rather sombre expression lit up.

'It won't take me long. The wagon is at the front.'

'Are you alone?' Laura asked, wondering if he'd be able to manage without help.

'Don't worry,' he said, reading her mind. 'I manage quite well by myself. I will knock on the door when I have finished.'

'All right.'

Laura didn't know whether to close the door on him or not, but when he walked away from her and round the side of the house, she decided it would be best if she did so.

She went back to the table but found she couldn't concentrate on her shopping list as she was waiting for Tom to reappear. He came round from the front several times, hauling huge sacks on his back.

When he had finished his arduous task he knocked on the door again. When Laura opened it a second time she saw that he was sweating profusely, leaning his hand against the wall at the side of the door.

'All done,' he said, breathing heavily.

'Thank you. Please come in.'

Tom entered the kitchen, standing just inside the open doorway so that Laura couldn't close it behind him.

'I'll get the money. Please, sit down.'

She indicated a kitchen chair but when she returned to the kitchen, Tom was still standing in the same place and the door was still open, letting in the cold, misty air. She handed him the money.

'I think that will be all right,' she said.

Tom nodded, pocketing the money without bothering to count it.

'Thank you, Miss March,' he said.

'Please, call me Laura, and, please, let me make you some tea.'

He waved his hand.

'No, no tea. That is not necessary.'

'But I want to,' Laura insisted.

It was the least she could do. She managed to shuffle her way round Tom and closed the back door with a firm click.

'There!' she announced. 'The kettle will be boiling in no time.'

As she busied herself she didn't look at Tom, but presently she heard him drawing out a chair and sitting at the table. She smiled to herself.

'Mr March always asks me to have tea and I always refuse, not because I am rude or ungrateful, you understand,' Tom said, 'but because it is not necessary to offer me tea.'

'I know it's not necessary, it's just nice.'

Laura put two mugs on the table, thinking he might prefer a mug to a cup. She made the tea and sat down, waiting for it to brew. She nearly asked if he would like a biscuit but knew instinctively that he would refuse politely.

He had his hands resting on the table and was looking down at them. Laura noticed his fingers were long and slender, not a labourer's hands at all and wondered what, if anything, he did for a living. She knew from what Ben had told her that his father worked at the mill in Browdale, but this did not mean, of course, that Tom did the same.

When she poured the tea, he waved aside her offer of milk.

'I prefer tea black, no milk, no sugar,' he said.

'With lemon perhaps?' Laura asked, knowing there wasn't a lemon in the house.

Tom smiled.

'No lemon, just black tea.'

He lifted the mug to his lips and took a long drink.

'Ah, very good,' he remarked.

He seemed to be relaxing, more at ease. Laura decided to try to find out more about him.

'My father told me you live at the big house,' she said.

'Is that its name?' he asked, looking puzzled.

'Well, no, not officially, but its always been called that by the locals.'

Tom nodded.

'Very appropriate. So many rooms, but we do not use them all.'

Laura knew the feeling though the manse was nowhere as big. She sat back in her chair, lifting up her own mug of tea.

'And how do you like living in Winford?'

'It is good. Nice people, kind people. They have made us most welcome, my parents and me. And Anton. He is my cousin.'

'Your father works at the mill, doesn't he?' Laura asked, knowing full well that he did.

'He has good job there. He is most grateful to be able to work.'

'And you?' she prompted.

'I am student, at your university in Leeds. I am mathematician.'

Tom swallowed the rest of his tea and stood up.

'Thank you for the tea. I will go now. My mother is expecting me back. She worries. She has no English so she sometimes feels isolated.'

Laura got up, too, wishing he would stay longer. There was so much she wanted to ask him, but she knew she couldn't. She thought Tom might resent too much prying, and rightly so. He probably knew what being interrogated was all about and she had no wish to upset him.

'I will see you next week,' Tom said, going towards the door.

'Oh, I hope before that,' Laura said.

'No, I don't think so. I have school and my mother — I stay and help her as much as I can. Goodbye, Laura.'

He gave a stiff bow and left. Laura ran from the kitchen into the front room, a room they hardly used, to look out of the window and watch him go. He walked quickly down the long path and the steps that led to the gate. His wagon was parked at the kerb. He hoisted himself into it, shut the door and drove off up the hill.

Laura returned slowly to the kitchen. So now she had met one of the people from the big house, and she liked Tom.

She sensed that he was rather shy and sensitive. She also imagined it must be very lonely for his mother if she didn't speak English. If Tom's father was away at the mill all day, and Tom was attending university, what did Anton do? It was quite possible that the mother spent a great deal of time alone. Perhaps, Laura thought, there might come a time when she would be able to coax Tom's mother to become part of the village community. She hoped so.

4

As she took her seat in the chapel on Sunday morning, Laura looked up into the gallery that ran along three sides of the building. There weren't many people up there, but Harry was one of them, sitting forward on the front row, his arms resting on the balcony edge, staring down at her. He saw that she had noticed him and lifted his hand in a slight wave.

She didn't wave back, but inclined her head slightly, then picked up her hymn book and studied the numbers on the board by the central pulpit. Laura was alone. She had seen that Shirley was not keen on the idea of going to church and neither Laura nor Ben had tried to force her.

The congregation was sparse and mixed, mostly middle-aged or elderly people with a handful of evacuees and their foster families, for the most part looking distinctly uncomfortable in the enforced stricture of Sunday best clothes. There would be considerably more worshippers at the six o'clock evening service and the afternoon Sunday School was always well-attended.

Laura could never remember Harry being at the chapel before. In fact he had been openly opposed to being there, declaring the roof would fall in if he should enter a house of prayer. But he was certainly here now. What was he up to? Laura found it difficult to concentrate on the service, knowing that Harry was above her, looking down, being able to keep his eye on her.

Ben March was a good preacher. Laura enjoyed listening to his sermons, but this morning her thoughts were flying and she was glad when the service ended. As normally happened, Ben moved to the doorway during the last strains of music after the Benediction and today was no exception. Laura lingered in her pew, fiddling with her gloves, having a word with the couple immediately in front of her. When she got to her feet she saw Harry standing talking to Ben, leaning heavily on his stick. Despite his injured leg, he must surely have taken the stairs from the gallery.

'Good morning, Laura,' he greeted her with a smile. 'Lovely morning, isn't it?'

'It certainly is.'

'You don't look particularly surprised to see me here.'

'Should I be?'

Why did he have to look so very handsome today? He was dressed in a crisp white shirt and dark blue tie, his hair under control for once.

'Now, now, you two, stop bickering,' Ben scolded.

He turned away to speak to Dr Waddington, the general practitioner who served all the bordering villages. Harry took hold of Laura's elbow in a firm grasp and led her outside into the sunshine.

'I'll come clean,' Harry began. 'There is a method in my madness. I wanted to speak to you and this seemed to be the best way to do it. You still don't have a telephone at the manse, I take it.'

'No. Dad was thinking of having one installed, I think, but then the war started and it seemed there were more important things to worry about.'

'Fair enough,' Harry said. 'Laura, would you come and have tea at the Hirams' this afternoon? There's something I need to discuss with you, well, a couple of things really. Geoffrey and his wife won't be there, by the way.'

Why was he telling her that? Did he deliberately want her to know they would be alone in the house together? What if they were? She wasn't afraid to meet him in such a situation. He saw her hesitation and rushed on.

'Please, Laura, I wouldn't ask you if it wasn't important. It concerns the evacuees, if you must know.'

'All right, I'll come,' she said.

Harry looked relieved.

'Thanks. About three thirty?'

Laura nodded.

Harry suddenly put the palm of his hand against her cheek, in a gentle and, to Laura, an intimate gesture. She jerked away from his touch.

'Oh, Laura, Laura, what am I going to do with you?' he said with a sigh.

Dr and Mrs Waddington walked past. Harry raised his hat politely to the doctor's wife and Laura took the opportunity to leave, hurrying along the drive between the ancient graves. This was ridiculous, she must try to control herself as far as Harry Lomax was concerned. She was acting like a schoolgirl. She would meet him that afternoon, discuss whatever business he had and steel herself not to respond to any of his banter. She must let him know, once and for all, so even he could understand, that she wasn't interested in his overtures.

The trouble was, she loved him. She felt miserable with love for him and even tea at the headmaster's house was going to prove an ordeal for her.

After Sunday dinner Shirley surprised both Laura and Ben.

'I think I'll go to Sunday School this afternoon,' she announced.

Laura and Ben looked at one another. Ben smiled.

'Splendid idea!' he cried. 'We can walk along there together.'

'Won't you be there, Laura?' Shirley asked, a slight doubt in her voice.

'No, Shirley, I can't. Perhaps I might start teaching Sunday School again next week, if that's all right by you, Dad.'

'Of course it is. We're always short of volunteers.'

Ben looked at Shirley.

'You'll be in my class. Who knows, in a few weeks' time, when you get used to everybody, we might put you in charge of some of the little ones.'

Shirley looked excited.

'Reading them Bible stories, supervising their picture colouring,' Ben went on.

80

'What a good idea,' Laura said. 'The kiddies love crayoning.'

'Do you mean it?'

Shirley's eyes glowed.

'I never say anything I don't mean,' Ben told her.

Laura told Ben about her meeting with Harry.

'Do you know what he has in mind?' she asked.

'Not a word. He hasn't said anything to me.'

Ben wisely said nothing about her agreeing to meet Harry. He had asked no questions about the other night when she met Harry at the station buffet and she had not volunteered any information. She preferred it that way.

She walked the short distance to the headmaster's house on the outskirts of the village, feeling more nervous with every step she took.

The house was a large, detached one, approached by a flight of steep, stone steps. The bay windows were bedecked with frilly white curtains and when

Harry opened the front door to Laura's knock, she stepped into an elegant hall, fragrant with the smell of furniture polish and fresh flowers. He showed her into the front parlour. Here, too, there was an over-abundance of flowers, ornaments and knick-knacks and family photographs.

A round table with a lacy white cloth had been placed in front of the fireplace where a coal fire burned cheerfully. Laura nearly groaned out loud when she saw the fare spread out on that table. There were dainty sandwiches, home-made cakes and fancy biscuits. Mrs Hiram must be a miracle worker if she could produce such a feast from her weekly rations!

'Sorry about all that,' Harry said. 'Millicent insisted.'

'So long as you don't expect me to eat any of it,' Laura told him. 'I'm still full from my dinner.'

'Not even a teeny, weeny cake?' Harry wheedled. 'I don't want to offend my hostess.'

Laura relented.

She sat down without invitation on a chair which seemed to swallow her up. Harry took the couch, sitting back, easing his bad leg across his other, looking for all the world as though he was settled there for the duration.

Oh, no, Laura thought, we don't want any cosy fireside scene.

'What was it you wanted to talk to me about, Harry?' she asked briskly.

He straightened up at her crisp tone.

'Straight to the point, eh?' he said with a grin.

'Of course.'

Harry laced his finger tips together.

'What do you think about running a weekly letter-writing class for the evacuees?'

Harry had done as she wanted and come straight to the point. Laura was surprised. This wasn't what she had expected, though she couldn't have said what she did expect.

'A letter-writing class?' she repeated.

Harry spoke eagerly, leaning towards her chair.

'Some of the children, such as Shirley, are very literate, some much less so, but I thought if every child who wanted to could write a weekly letter home it might help them, and I'm sure their parents would welcome such letters. Even the very young ones can be encouraged to write simple notes, or send a drawing perhaps. Left to their own devices I doubt whether many would bother getting down to writing letters, but in a group situation, with each child encouraging the other, I think it might work.'

'And you want me to be in charge of this group?' Laura asked, quickly warming to the idea.

'Yes, that's the general plan. I thought perhaps Saturday morning might be a good time. Geoffrey says you can use one of the classrooms. Are you free on Saturday mornings, Laura?'

She smiled, relaxing for the first time since she had arrived.

'I can be free whenever you need me, Harry,' she said.

'Good. Then that's settled.'

Harry stood up.

'I'll make the tea now, shall I?'

'Is that it?'

'Well, yes, short and to the point. Isn't that the way you wanted it?'

To her chagrin, Laura felt herself blushing.

'Couldn't you simply have asked me outside the chapel this morning?'

'I could, but I didn't want to. Anyway there's . . . '

Laura cut in angrily, getting to her feet.

'So you've got me here under false pretences then?'

'Oh, for goodness' sake, Laura, stop being so childish,' Harry burst out.

Laura calmed down. She was doing precisely what she had told herself she wouldn't do, getting involved, getting upset.

'And if you'd let me finish my sentence,' Harry went on, 'I was going to mention my other idea.'

'And what's that?'

Laura sat down again, wanting to kick herself.

'Over a cup of tea,' Harry said cheerfully. 'Won't be long.'

When he left the room, Laura stared miserably at the array of food. She didn't want the tea, and she still didn't want any of the food. She sat there, wishing she hadn't come. Harry's idea was brilliant and she supposed she did want to hear what else he had in mind, but not like this, the two of them in close proximity in a room that was becoming too overpoweringly warm.

Harry returned. He was pleased with himself, she could see that.

'This other idea,' he began, setting the teapot on the already overcrowded table. 'Will you pour by the way?'

Laura was glad to. The delicate, rose-patterned teapot looked most awkward in Harry's large hands.

'You were saying?' she prompted him.

'Oh, yes.'

Harry resumed his seat on the couch.

'I thought it would be rather nice to have a party, a sort of welcoming party for the new children, with as many people who want to come, of course. And I also thought it would be a golden opportunity to invite the Polish family along.'

Laura remembered what Tom Bronowski had said about his mother and wondered if they would be happy with this idea, but she didn't say anything. She handed Harry a cup of tea.

'It would require a lot of planning, a lot of help,' she said.

'But if we organised it together, Laura, you and I, I'm sure it would be possible. And I thought, to give us the time we need, we could fix it for November the fifth.'

'Bonfire night!'

'Exactly. I think I know where I can get hold of some indoor sparklers and the children could make a Guy Fawkes.

We could have bonfire toffee, parkin, baked potatoes, the lot. No actual bonfire, of course, but that wouldn't matter, would it?'

Harry was fired with enthusiasm and Laura was becoming infected, too.

'Don't forget everything is rationed, Harry,' she reminded him, hating to sound like a killjoy.

'Oh, we'll manage, with everybody chipping in.'

Harry refused to let a little matter like being at war stand in his way.

Laura put down her half-drunk tea. Neither of them had touched poor Mrs Hiram's goodies, but Harry hadn't seemed to notice.

'Let's get it all down on paper,' she said. 'Is there a table we can use?'

'In the kitchen,' Harry said.

So they went there and Harry produced an exercise book and a couple of pencils. They sat close together at the table, each with a sheet from the exercise book in front of them. Laura wasn't aware that Harry's face was close to hers, that their fingers were a hair's breadth away from each other. They were both too intent on scribbling their notes, making their plans, until they both looked up together, catching the expression in each other's eyes.

'Laura,' Harry said, his voice hoarse.

Unthinkingly, Laura put her hand over Harry's, feeling the shape of his knuckles, the texture of his skin.

'Oh, Harry!' she breathed.

They kissed, gently at first, then they both stood up together, their arms entwined. When they parted, Laura rested her head on Harry's shoulder and it felt so right, so proper. She didn't want to move. Her anger had gone, her distrust evaporated. This was Harry, the man she loved, and she wanted to stay in his arms for ever.

5

It was crisp, cold and clear on November the fifth. She remembered such nights from her childhood, the excitement, the thrill of being allowed to stay up late.

Of course, this year it would be slightly different. There would be no fire, no fireworks except the few indoor ones Harry had produced miraculously. But all the other ingredients would be there. Willing hands had helped to decorate the school hall with balloons and paper chains. The children had joined forces to create the most wonderful outsize Guy.

There were baked potatoes, dug from people's backyards and allotments, cooked at home and brought in cloth-covered dishes to the school hall; homemade rich, dark, sticky parkin, and Miss Cook had managed to provide the traditional bonfire toffee.

Shirley was dancing with excitement by the time the three of them left the manse, wrapped up well against the cold. She had been beside herself all day and was now gazing proudly at the dish of ginger biscuits she had made all by herself, with a little help from Laura!

'I've never been to a bonfire party before,' she said, pulling her beret on to her head.

As they were leaving the house, Ben had one of his coughing fits, holding his gloved hand over his mouth.

'Are you all right, Dad?' Laura asked anxiously.

Ben waited till his coughing had subsided.

'Oh, yes, it's just when the cold air hits me.'

Laura was worried about him. To her mind, he hadn't looked too well these past few days but he had insisted on being as much involved with the party preparations as everybody else. Laura wished he would let up, but she knew it would be useless to ask him to do so. She could only make sure she kept a clean house, a warm house, as good a table as she could under wartime conditions and make sure he never went out without a woolly scarf wound around his neck.

They walked in a line towards the school which was near the end of Beech Road, linking arms, not needing to use the torch on such a clear, moonlit night. A bomber's moon, Laura had heard it called and thought briefly of the planes defending the skies, the ground forces and sailors at sea, all doing their bit to keep the enemy at bay.

But tonight was a time for happiness. This was the children's night and Laura knew every adult would do their very best to ensure that each child had a good time. No lights shone from windows, of course, but once inside the school, the excitement and anticipation were evident. Children were running up and down, waving streamers, shouting, wearing homemade paper hats. Long trestle tables had been set out with chairs all round the walls of the hall. Guy Fawkes had pride of place at the far end on the raised platform, perched on a chair, resplendent.

Laura looked all round eagerly for Harry, but she couldn't see him. She felt a tingle of disappointment. She had thought he would be one of the first there. Things were going really well between them. They never spoke about the past, only of the future. However, it wasn't long though before he arrived. He was not alone. Laura recognised Tom Bronowski at once and the older couple with him must be his parents, Peter and Anya. This was the first time Laura had seen Tom's parents. Only Tom's cousin, Anton, was absent.

Laura left the drinks' table and went across to greet the newcomers. She was pleased, though a bit embarrassed, when Harry bent to kiss her cheek. The gesture seemed to say that they were together. She liked that.

'Laura,' Harry began, 'I'd like you to meet Peter and Anya Bronowski. You know their son, Tom, of course. Mr and Mrs Bronowski, this is Laura March, Ben March's daughter.'

'How do you do?' Laura said, shaking the couple by the hand.

Peter was tall and broad-shouldered, with smooth, almost white hair. His wife, Anya, was much smaller than he was and had a motherly face. Her hair was dark, liberally flecked with grey, plaited around her head. She smiled shyly as she shook hands with Laura and said something in Polish, but Peter spoke very good English.

'I am very pleased to meet you, Miss March,' he said. 'I know your father quite well. I am sorry you have seen so little of us at such events as these. Perhaps in the future we might become more neighbourly.'

Laura smiled.

'You're very welcome, Mr Bronowski.'

She turned to Tom who had so far said nothing.

'Good evening, Tom.'

He inclined his head.

'Good evening, Laura.'

'Well, come and join the party!' Harry cried.

Anya Bronowski held out a small, flat parcel, wrapped in a white cloth, speaking again in Polish, nodding and smiling shyly. Peter explained.

'My wife has brought some home-made bread, her speciality.'

He sounded very proud of her as Laura took the proffered gift.

'Thank you. Thank you very much,' she said.

A game of musical chairs had come to an end and someone had decided it was time to eat, so a hungry horde of youngsters was quickly descending on the tables. The Bronowskis had gone to sit down and Ben, free for a few moments from his self-appointed task of children's entertainer, crossed to speak to them. Harry and Laura found themselves alone. He put his arm around her waist.

'You look beautiful, Laura,' he whispered.

'Thank you.'

'I wish I could take you in my arms and kiss you.'

'Don't you dare!' she warned him. 'And where's Anton, by the way?'

'He declined to be present,' Harry said. 'Excruciatingly shy is Anton apparently.'

'You've met him then?'

'Briefly. He can speak English, when he wants to, but he doesn't say very much at all really.'

Shirley came towards them, munching on a baked potato.

'Hello, Harry,' she said, between hot mouthfuls.

Harry looked stern.

'Now, Shirley, what have I told you about using my Christian name? I'm Mr Lomax to you now, just the same as everybody else.'

'Sorry, Mr Lomax,' Shirley said with

a grin, waltzing away again to join her friends.

'Cheeky young madam,' Harry said but Laura could tell he wasn't really cross. 'It's my own fault,' he explained. 'I know Shirley's mother quite well. Her father died about two years ago, and that's when I started visiting the family. All the children call me 'Arry.'

'Funny how your Cockney accent comes and goes,' Laura declared.

'Let's dance,' Harry suggested.

Laura stared at him.

'How can you possibly dance with your bad leg? No offence meant, of course.'

'None taken, and if I can't manage a simple dance, I'll stand hanging as my old dad used to say.'

'Right, come on,' Laura challenged him.

Mrs Lawton was now playing the music for a barn dance. As Laura and Harry joined the others in a circle she was remembering what a good dancer Harry had once been, but for now she threw herself wholeheartedly into the bonfire party and she knew she was the happiest girl there that night.

She managed to talk to Tom at one stage, even asked him to dance, though she knew that wasn't very good etiquette. Tom laughed and shook his head.

'I cannot dance. I would only embarrass myself and tread on your toes, Laura. Sit and talk to me, if you like,' he suggested.

Harry was busy organising Blind Man's Buff whilst Ben was engaged in earnest conversation with Peter Bronowski, Anya sitting at his side, looking happy and content to watch the proceedings around her. Laura took the chair next to Tom.

'This is good,' Tom said, nodding in the general direction of the festivities. 'I must admit I do not know of your Guy Fawkes' tradition. Oh, I know of the Gunpowder Plot, of course, but not that your country is still celebrating such an event, if celebrating is the right word to use.'

Laura laughed.

'We're an odd bunch, we English people,' she said, 'but this is nothing compared to what a real bonfire party is like, when we have it outside, build a big fire and put the Guy on top.'

'Then set fire to him, I suppose?'

'That's right.'

'Poor old Guy Fawkes. It is the war which prevents the outdoor party?'

'Yes, the war.'

'But up here in Yorkshire, you are fortunate, are you not, to be away from the bombing? I know your big cities, Sheffield, Manchester, even Leeds where I study are at risk, but here, surely you are safe?'

'I hope so,' Laura said fervently.

She wondered if this was the opportunity she needed to get him to talk about himself, but it seemed not. Tom smiled at her.

'I think perhaps I might try some of that delicious supper now. Will you join me, please?'

Laura was happy to comply.

The evening wore on but at last it was over. Remains of food, and there wasn't much, were distributed amongst the ones with children. Decorations and paper hats and poor old Guy Fawkes were gathered together, ready for disposal and the revellers began to wend their different ways homeward.

Shirley was half asleep, but Laura was very much awake, feeling like an excited child. Harry walked beside her, holding her hand.

At the gate to the manse Ben said to Shirley, 'Come on, love, let's get you to bed.'

Laura lingered in the open gateway with Harry.

'See you later, Harry,' Ben said. 'I'll leave the door open, darling.'

This was to Laura and she knew her father understood her need to be alone with Harry for a few moments. Shirley was too tired to notice and went willingly with Ben into the house. Harry wasted no time. Once they were safely alone, he gathered Laura into his arms and gave her a long kiss.

'You know I'm in love with you, don't you, Laura?' he said softly.

'Yes, and I love you, too.'

'Some day, in the not-too-distant future, I want to make you my wife. It isn't possible now, my main concern being to take care of the children. Their parents are relying on me. You do understand, don't you?'

'I understand,' Laura told him.

'But when this ghastly war is over . . . '

This was what they must all hope for, a speedy end to the war. Laura would be patient. Their love would last for a million years, so what did a few of those years matter if that was what it took.

The next morning, Saturday, was another letter-writing meeting and Shirley always went along to the meeting with Laura. When they came back to the manse, Ben had some news for them.

'I've had two visitors whilst you were out,' he said. 'Tom was one. He brought the wood, of course, though I did tell him at the bonfire party that we had enough wood to last for another three weeks at least. However, I think the real reason he came was to issue an invitation to dinner tonight.'

'Tonight?' Laura repeated.

'Can I go as well?' Shirley piped in.

Ben smiled at her.

'Well, I was wondering about that, so I popped out to see Mrs Walshaw. Wouldn't you prefer to go there for tea and then spend the night, too?'

Mrs Walshaw had been giving tea parties for one child or another at her house. Now it was Shirley's turn and she was plainly delighted.

'Oh, yes please,' she said.

'I thought you'd say that,' Ben remarked.

Although there were a few hours before Shirley would be leaving for the Walshaws, she decided to run upstairs and pack whatever she needed. Thanks to Laura, she had quite a wardrobe by now and was immensely proud of all her new clothes.

'Are there just the two of us going, Dad?' Laura asked.

'No, Harry as well. According to Tom it was Anya who made the suggestion. So being at the Guy Fawkes' party was a very good thing.'

'I'm quite looking forward to visiting the big house,' Laura admitted. 'I've never actually been inside it. And who was your second visitor?'

Ben sat down in his fireside chair.

'Well, you won't believe it but I had a member of the military here.'

Surprised, Laura, too, sat down.

'Go on,' she urged.

'He was a Platoon Commander from an engineering regiment, a young, very smart lieutenant. He asked me if I would be willing to have some of his men billeted in the crypt for a couple of weeks.'

'What on earth for?'

'Well, he didn't go into the reasons, Laura, understandably. He made a simple, unequivocal request and of course I said yes, I would be delighted.'

How like her father, Laura thought! Just recovering from a serious illness, a busy parish to run, to a certain extent the well-being of twenty young evacuees to consider but he would never dream of turning anyone away who needed his help!

'They'll be no bother to us,' Ben went on. 'I showed him the crypt, what a state it's in and he said, no matter, they'd have it sorted out in no time. They'll be bringing all their own gear, camp beds and the like and be entirely self-sufficient.'

'When are they coming?'

'In the next few days. I couldn't say no, could I, dear?'

Laura smiled.

'Of course you couldn't. I'm glad there's the room for them.'

Water wouldn't be a problem as it was laid on in the crypt and there were water closets and a washroom of sorts, but no cooking facilities. However, Laura didn't think that would bother servicemen who were used to eating whatever came to hand out of billy cans.

Despite avowing that the soldiers' presence would not affect their lives at all, Ben went to his study after lunch to put pen to paper and draw up some sort of assistance plan, should it be needed, as Laura had known he would.

Once Shirley had left for the Walshaws, insisting on going the short distance alone, Laura decided she would go into town and try to find a new outfit for the coming evening. She still had clothing coupons left. She still hadn't done anything about getting her trunk from Scotland, though she did think her father had more or less accepted she was here to stay.

She took the trolley bus for the four-mile journey. Even in wartime, buses were fairly regular.

As usual on Saturday afternoons, the town centre was crowded. Usually Laura was content to window shop, as many people did, and perhaps go into the Kingsway café for a cup of tea. If a tea dance was in progress, she would sit and watch the dancers, envying them their grace and skill.

The most likely shop to buy what she wanted was Kayes' department store, one of the largest and plushest in Bletchfield. Laura decided to go there first and started walking down King Street.

Ahead of her, among the thronged shoppers, she suddenly caught a glimpse of Harry. Even though he was wearing a hat she knew it was him and she quickened her pace but as she drew nearer she saw it couldn't be Harry because he wasn't carrying a stick and though he did appear to have a peculiar gait, he certainly didn't have Harry's very pronounced limp.

Laura slowed her steps. No need in rushing if it wasn't him, but as she drew nearer to the store, the man ahead stopped and turned to his right, as though uncertain of where he was heading. And it was Harry! He had no limp, no stick. He was as able bodied as anyone. She started to run towards him and when she drew level, he looked round and saw her. She saw by the expression on his face that he was immediately suffused with guilt.

'Laura,' he said, just the one word, terse, as though she were a stranger.

'Why are you just pretending to be lame, Harry?' she asked him directly.

'I'm not.'

'Yes, you are. You're living a lie. Why?'

'I am who I say I am. I'm Harry Lomax, teacher of English. I'm thirty-two years old and six feet . . . '

'Oh, stop it!' she cried.

'We can't talk here,' Harry said.

'All I want to know is where your limp has gone and your stick. Why are you living this ridiculous charade?'

She knew the answer before he told her, or thought she did. It must be some deliberate ploy to keep from serving on active duty, but it couldn't be. Not her Harry, not the man she loved. But could she love him, a man like that who pretended to be lame to keep him out of active service?

'There's a park near here, if I remember,' Harry said. 'We'll talk there.'

He gripped her shoulder and the only way she could escape would be to make a scene. He marched her up the street and to the small park where there were benches and a memorial to the fallen of World War One. Harry sat on a bench directly in front of this memorial. Laura remained standing.

'Sit down, Laura, please.'

Harry sounded angry now.

'I'm sorry you saw me, Laura,' he said in a calmer voice when she sat beside him. 'I never intended for you to see me without my stick.'

'Without your disguise, you mean,' Laura shot at him.

He ignored that remark.

'I try not to step out of character but it isn't easy, so when I'm alone, naturally, I drop the phoney limp though I have some degree of lameness, I'm sure you must have noticed.'

She had. What difference did that make? It wasn't enough of a problem to stop him being called up. He was a complete phoney. Laura wanted to burst into tears but wouldn't give him the satisfaction of seeing her cry.

'I'd like to say I can explain everything, Laura, but I can't, not at the present time. You'll just have to trust me. You said you loved me. Love and trust go hand in hand, don't they, or at least they do in my book.'

'I'm tired of you saying that to me, Harry. What about you trusting me for a change and telling me the truth? I'm not a child, you know. You only force me to believe the worst about you, always the worst, like when you left me all those years ago. You tell me lies, Harry, nothing but lies.'

'No, Laura, I have never told you a lie,' Harry insisted.

'No? You said you'd hurt your leg in a car crash. Wasn't that a lie?'

'It was more a distortion of the truth than a lie. Are you going to expose me now, Laura?'

'Why shouldn't I? Isn't it what you deserve?'

'If you say so.'

Suddenly he sounded weary and despite her anger Laura felt the love she still had for him, fool that she was, stir inside her.

'But I can only beg you not to do so,' he said.

She looked at him. His expression was so intrinsically honest that she found herself wavering. Harry went on.

'At the risk of repeating myself, I want you once again to trust me, Laura. My love for you is genuine and it always has been. I wouldn't lie to you about that, never about that.'

He didn't try to touch her and for that she was grateful. She stood up.

'Let me leave alone,' she said. 'Please don't follow me.'

Laura walked away from him, aware that he was watching her. Tears were now running down her cheeks, unchecked. She was consumed by doubts, suspicions. She didn't know which way to turn. She would go straight back home, leave her shopping for another day. She needed to shut herself away for a while so that when evening came she could put on a brave face, pretend everything was all right and smile at Harry across a dinner table. It wouldn't be easy deceiving her father but she had to try.

★ ★ ★

There were six of them around the table in the vast dining-room of the big house. The table was elaborately laid with fine cutlery and china and glassware, items which had probably travelled with the Polish people from their homeland. Laura could only speculate about the true reasons for their exodus. It was plain to see that they were people of means.

Laura was sitting next to her father with Peter on her right, at the head of the table. Directly opposite Laura sat Anton Chezyck. She was surprised on seeing him for the first time that he did not resemble any of the other members of his family. He had long, floppy fair hair which constantly fell across his brow and though tall, was also slenderly built and, as Harry had said, he was very quiet. However, Anton, she observed, seemed to watch her constantly as they sat at the table and the expression in his blue eyes was bold rather than shy. A strange young man, she thought.

Harry sat next to Anton. He was his usual charming self, but Laura avoided looking at him as much as possible. Because they were guests in someone's house for the first time she did not think her quietness would be amiss.

Tom was placed next to Harry and Anya, gentle, unassuming, sat opposite her husband, when she wasn't hurrying to and from the kitchen to bring in, first, steaming bowls of carrot soup, and afterwards the main course in a huge tureen which turned out to be stew.

Because Anya spoke no English, general conversation was proving to be a little difficult, though Peter and his son deferred constantly to her in her own language.

'I hope none of you has eaten much during the day,' Peter said with a smile. 'My wife will expect the tureen to be wiped clean and then, of course, there will be her famous plum cake to enjoy.'

Harry groaned and touched his stomach.

'I'm full up already.'

Once more Tom translated for his mother. She laughed, a lovely sound. Only Anton didn't join in the conversation, unless a remark was addressed directly to him. When the meal was finally over, when no-one could possibly eat another morsel, Peter stood up from the table.

'Coffee and brandy, I think, in the drawing-room,' he said expansively.

'Sounds good,' Harry said.

'I'd love coffee,' Ben said. 'It's such a rare treat these days, but no brandy, thank you. I'm a teetotaller. No offence, but I am a Methodist minister and as such I don't drink. But, of course, I wouldn't dream of censoring you for enjoying your after-dinner brandies. What about you, Laura, dear?'

He winked at her and Laura blushed.

'Well, I did pick up the bad habit in Scotland, Dad,' she admitted.

'In moderation, I take it?' Ben asked with mock severity.

'Naturally.'

They moved to the drawing-room, where the fire was still blazing and the curtains drawn against the dark and cold outside. Laura sat on a wide, deep sofa and was glad when Harry took a chair away from her. Tom came and sat by Laura.

'So you have lived in Scotland?' he asked. 'A beautiful, wild country, I am told.'

'Very beautiful,' Laura said.

'Did you work there?'

'Yes. I was a receptionist in a hotel on Loch Long.'

'Was?' Ben said, puzzled. 'I thought you still were.'

'Not any more, Dad. I'm home for good.'

She spoke lightly and she knew Ben would not challenge her further, not in front of their hosts. Later, perhaps . . .

'That is good,' Peter said, 'to be with your father. But do you not have a mother?'

'Laura's mother died when she was very small,' Ben said.

'Oh, I see.'

Laura hardly remembered her mother and knew her father thought of her only with tenderness and affection, not sadness or grief after all these years.

'I am glad,' Peter went on, 'that I have my son with me, and Anton, too, of course.'

He nodded towards his nephew, standing at the back of the room, nursing his brandy glass as though he wasn't really part of the proceedings.

'When we first came to England Anton did not come and I worried for his safety, but then he decided to join us. That made us very happy, especially my Anya, whose sister was Anton's mother. Eva died a few years ago.'

It was the first time Laura had heard any personal details about the Polish family. Anya came into the room at that moment with a wheeled trolley. As Anya started to pour the coffee, Anton put down his brandy glass and gave his peculiar little bow to the assembled company.

'I will excuse myself now. It has been my pleasure to meet you all. Good-night,' he said and he was gone, closing the door carefully behind him.

Anya looked upset and spoke rapidly in Polish to her husband. Peter came to her, patting her shoulder gently.

'I must apologise for my nephew's rudeness,' he said.

'That's all right,' Ben said. 'No doubt he has things to do.'

Tom made a loud, snorting noise.

'He had nothing to do, nothing except to dream, that is.'

Peter spoke to Tom sharply and an awkward silence then seemed to develop, which Tom eventually broke.

'Tell me more about Scotland, Laura,' he said.

She was glad to do so, and she took the opportunity to ask, 'And what's it like in your country?'

Tom and Peter looked at one another and instantly Laura regretted her thoughtless remark.

'I'm sorry,' she stammered. 'I wasn't thinking. It must be awful in Poland at the moment.'

'For many it is, yes,' Peter agreed. 'We are among the fortunate.'

He said no more on the subject and, once again, Laura was left to speculate on the reasons for their being driven from their homeland.

In a light voice Ben said, 'Laura tells me, Tom, that you are a student at Leeds University. A clever fellow by all accounts. Maths, isn't it?'

'Yes, mathematics.'

'Never my favourite subject,' Harry admitted, speaking for what must be the first time since they came into the room.

'Tom attended Heidelberg University, in Germany, before we came to England,' Peter said proudly.

'A very beautiful city,' Tom said.

The word, Germany, seemed to hang in the air, till Harry said with a laugh, 'I know the story of The Student Prince, of course, and Romberg's beautiful music.'

Everybody laughed as he burst into song. Harry had a surprisingly good voice. Laura wanted to tell him so, but she hesitated to address any direct remark to him. She must avoid him at all costs and, later, when they left the big house, she made a point of walking on the opposite side of her father to Harry and left the two men to make conversation, which they did.

Now that they were away from the

house and there wasn't such a need for sensitivity, Harry and Ben talked about the war. Laura knew her father spent a lot of time listening to the wireless, and he read the newspapers.

At the bottom of the hill, they stopped. Harry would take a different route from there.

'Thanks for your company, Harry,' Ben said, patting Harry's shoulder.

'It's been a good evening, hasn't it?' Harry remarked. 'Well, good-night. Good-night, Laura.'

'Good-night, Harry,' they both said together.

As Harry walked off into the darkness, Laura watched him go, listening to his uneven footsteps echoing through the silent night.

'Well, well,' Ben said as they headed for Station Lane, 'what's the matter with you then? You weren't yourself tonight.'

'There's nothing the matter with me, Dad.'

'Oh, come, come. Last night, you and

Harry were in each other's arms on the doorstep, and didn't you say things were good between you?'

'Things change, Dad.'

Laura didn't want to talk about it.

'And I take it that you want me to mind my own business.'

Relenting, Laura pushed her arm through Ben's.

'Oh, Dad, I'm sorry, but I can't talk about it now. Let's leave it that Harry and I aren't seeing eye to eye at the moment.'

'Fair enough,' he said as they'd reached the manse.

As he inserted the key in the front door Ben said, 'And don't you want to talk about your reasons for giving up your job, either?'

'Isn't it enough to say I want to be here with you, Dad? I'm not saying you're an invalid, you're obviously not, not now, but I didn't know how bad you were when I came home, did I? Let me spoil you for a while. I like doing that. Later, I'll probably get another job.'

Ben kissed her.

'Who am I to argue? Since when have you heeded a word I've said?'

Laura laughed, stepping into the dark hall whilst her father closed and locked the door behind them.

'Surely I'm not as bad as that,' she protested.

The tense moment had passed. Laura had managed to divert the conversation away from her and Harry, and it seemed as though her father had accepted the situation about her job.

It was late and they decided to go straight to bed, but Laura couldn't sleep. She was re-living the evening at the big house, what had been said, the strangeness of Anton Chezyck, but mostly she was thinking about Harry. To have been so long in his company and hardly say a word to one another was hard to take. Just at present she couldn't envisage a time when they would ever be able to be at ease with each other. She knew she would find it

121

intolerable watching him keep up the pretence about his leg.

Eventually, she slept but it was still dark and no time seemed to have elapsed when she was awoken by a loud banging at the front door. She was out of bed in seconds and was halfway down the stairs when Ben appeared on that landing.

'Who on earth can that be at this hour?' he said in a sleepy voice.

Laura unlocked the door. She gave a gasp of shock when she saw Mrs Bronowski standing there, a coat thrown over her nightdress, slippers on her feet, her hair hanging in a heavy plait over her shoulder.

'Mrs Bronowski! What happened?' Laura asked.

Ben had joined her by now and Mrs Bronowski rushed towards him, grasping his arms, looking up at him, her face wild with terror.

'Peter! Peter!' she cried, then burst into tears.

Ben looked at Laura.

'Something's happened to Peter,' he said. 'Get my coat, Laura. I'm going up there.'

'But what about Tom and Anton? Aren't they there?'

'Obviously not or Mrs Bronowski wouldn't have come here, would she?'

Ben was scrambling into his overcoat. Anya was still crying, but she had allowed Laura to put an arm around her shaking shoulders.

'Shall I keep her here, Dad?' Laura asked.

'I think it best, till I find out what's happened.'

Ben put his hat on and went out into the night. Laura took Anya into the living-room, sat her down and went to try to revive the dying embers of the fire, which had gone down really low.

Anya Bronowski was now sitting, moaning gently, rocking herself, her arms clasped across her chest.

6

Tom burst into the hospital waiting-room, followed closely by Harry. Laura leaped to her feet and Harry caught hold of both her hands.

'Laura, my dear! Are you all right?'

Despite the animosity and distrust she felt towards him, Laura was so glad that Harry was there. She had phoned him from the hospital, thankful that there was a phone at his lodgings. It was three in the morning by then and she was full of apologies for rousing him in the middle of the night.

'Harry,' she began, 'it's Laura here.'

'Laura? What's the matter? Is your father all right?'

'Yes. It isn't my father,' and she went on to tell him about Anya's visit to the house, and what Ben had discovered when he went to the big house.

'Peter was unconscious. Well, he still

is. Concussion, the doctor says. He was lying on the floor with a wound to his head.'

'Had he fallen?'

'We don't know. Neither Tom nor Anton was there. Harry, can you go up to the house, please? Perhaps one of them has come back by now.'

'Of course,' Harry said. 'What about Anya? Is she all right?'

'Yes, she's here. She's very distressed, naturally. They managed to find an interpreter for her, a Polish priest from the Roman Catholic church of Our Lady of Sorrows.'

'Tell me all about it when I get there,' Harry said. 'I'm on my way.'

'Will you get a taxi?' Laura asked.

'I'll borrow Geoffrey's car. It'll be quicker.'

Laura had an agonising wait. Her father and Anya were still at Peter's bedside. The priest was also there. Laura didn't know what they would have done without him.

But now, Harry was there, with poor

Tom, looking pale and strained.

'What happened? Did someone break into the house?' Tom asked.

Laura sat down again but the two men remained standing.

'I don't know,' she said. 'All I know is that your mother awoke in the night and Peter wasn't there. She called out for him but there was no answer so she went looking for him. She eventually found him in your room, Tom, lying out on the floor, unconscious and wounded. That's when she also discovered that both you and Anton weren't in the house.'

Tom sat down abruptly, resting his head in his hands.

'We'd had an argument, Anton and I,' he began. 'A stupid, pointless argument. We're always arguing, I'm afraid. Anton is my cousin but we do not really get on with one another. It started because I told Anton what I thought of him for walking out on our guests so rudely. I accused him of forever walking out in one way or another. My mother gets upset because she never knows where Anton is. Sometimes he is away for days at a time.'

'Doesn't he have a job?' Harry asked.

'He calls himself a poet,' Tom said. 'I call him The Dreamer and he hates that. He uses his creativity to get out of doing anything worthwhile. He never chops wood or does any other menial task. He never wields anything heavier than a pen. I am ashamed to say that we nearly came to blows and I knew I had to get out of the house. First I went and cut down some branches and chopped some logs, until I was physically exhausted but much calmer inside. Then I went for a walk. I had only just returned when you came, Harry. I found the house deserted.'

'So Anton had gone out, too,' Harry mused.

'Yes, but I doubt if Anton will return for quite some time.'

Ben appeared in the doorway of the waiting-room, looking very tired.

Tom leaped to his feet.

'How is Father?' he asked.

'Still unconscious, I'm afraid. He has surfaced temporarily for maybe a minute at a time, but that's all.'

'Can I see him?'

'Of course. I'll take you there, and, Tom, please don't be alarmed by the sight of the priest. He is there to act as interpreter for your mother, not because your father is in a critical condition.'

Tom gave a grim sort of smile and he and Ben left the room. There was a long silence.

Then Laura said, 'Thanks for coming, Harry.'

'That's all right.'

Harry came and sat by her.

'I don't know what to think about this business,' he admitted. 'Was it an attempted burglary or what? And what was Peter doing in Tom's room in the middle of the night? Was he dressed, do you know?'

'Yes, he was. Mrs Bronowski was very

concerned that her husband had never been to bed. Apparently she retired soon after we left and wasn't aware that Tom and Anton had left the house. I didn't say anything in front of Tom, but there was a claw hammer by Mr Bronowski's side.'

'Was he struck by that?' Harry asked, alarmed.

'I don't know. I suppose it's possible.'

'Have the police been informed?'

Laura looked at him in alarm.

'No. Do you think that's necessary?'

'Of course it is, if Peter's been attacked.'

'But that's up to Tom, isn't it? We can't do it.'

'No, I suppose not.'

Ben came back.

'Tom and his mother are staying a while longer, though Mrs Bronowski is totally exhausted and needs to get some rest. The priest has left.'

Ben rubbed his eyes. Laura got up and touched his arm gently.

'Dad, you need to get some rest as well,' she said.

He smiled at her.

'Yes, I suppose you're right. What should we do now, Harry?'

'I was thinking we should inform the police. If Peter was hit with a claw hammer . . . '

Ben looked horrified.

'But, he wasn't. Whatever that hammer was doing there, it certainly wasn't used as a weapon. The doctor seems to think Peter was struck from behind by a hand or a fist and that he only got the head wound when he fell, probably knocked against something. It was the blow that caused his concussion.'

'It's still an attack,' Harry said.

'I know but I think we should wait till Peter comes round fully so he can tell us exactly what happened,' Ben argued.

'That's if he knows,' Harry persisted.

Laura was feeling confused, scared and also very tired. She doubted if she would be able to sleep for what was left of the night, but she dearly wanted to be able to lie down and rest her head on the pillows.

'Shall we go home?' she suggested. 'Tom is here now. He'll take care of his mother.'

'Perhaps I should persuade her to go home with us,' Harry said.

'I don't think she will,' Ben remarked, 'not until she is sure Peter's going to be all right.'

'In that case, I'll give you two a lift back.'

'Thanks, Harry,' Ben said gratefully.

The roads were deserted. Ben sat in the front of the car by Harry and Laura in the back. She noticed the confident way Harry drove. She hadn't even known until tonight that Harry could drive. She realised at that moment there was so much about Harry she didn't know and now fresh doubts were beginning to creep into her mind. Yes, he was living a lie as far as his bad leg was concerned. Yes, he had tried to deceive her on more than one occasion, but why? That was the question she must ask herself.

He couldn't be a coward. He was too

strong a person for that. He had begged her to trust him but she had turned away from him, unable to do so, but tonight, in the hospital waiting-room, without touching one another, without any words of love passing between them, Laura had felt a strong closeness to Harry. If he could tell her the truth about himself, he would. She mustn't turn away from him because he wasn't prepared to do so. He needed her, she was sure of that. In the confines of the car, there wasn't much Laura could do to change the current situation, but once they arrived at the manse, after her father had left the car, she leaned towards Harry.

'I want to trust you, Harry,' she whispered. 'I love you so very much.'

He reached round and caught her hand for a brief moment. She could see him smiling in the darkness.

'Laura, I love you, too. Please, try to believe in me. I won't let you down. You have my word on that.'

Impulsively she kissed his cheek.

'Good-night, Harry,' she said.

She watched him drive away before joining her father at the door.

'I don't want to pry, darling,' Ben said, 'but is everything all right again between you and Harry?'

'I hope so, Dad, I hope so.' Laura sighed. 'I can't say any more, not yet.'

★ ★ ★

Tom came round to the manse early on Monday afternoon. Although he said almost at once that his father had regained consciousness, he still looked worried.

'That's splendid news,' Ben said.

'Of course it is,' Tom agreed, 'but my father is not himself. He turns away from me. He averts his eyes. I cannot understand why.'

Neither could Laura. She knew that Peter and Tom were very close.

'Perhaps it's after-shock,' Ben suggested. 'He is feeling better, isn't he?'

'He seems to have no after-effects

apart from a sore head. He was sitting up in bed when we arrived at the hospital this morning. He kissed and hugged my mother, but when I tried to embrace him he pulled away and spoke to me in an abrupt voice, as though he did not know me.'

'Was he able to tell you what happened?' Ben asked.

'No, he said he couldn't remember either what happened before he was hit or afterwards.'

'Well, there you are then! He's got amnesia. You'll have to make allowances, Tom, give him time,' Ben said.

'If he knew my mother, why would he not know me?' Tom persisted.

Ben could say nothing to that. It was strange. Laura felt sorry for Tom who looked so downhearted.

'What about Anton? Has he returned?' she asked.

'No, no sign of him, but that does not worry me. It is not unusual for him to leave without a word to anyone, especially after he and I have been involved in a disagreement.'

'And did your father mention Anton at all?'

'Yes, he asked where he was.'

This seemed to make the situation even stranger. Both Ben and Laura tried to put Tom at his ease and Laura invited him and his mother to tea but Tom declined.

'That is very kind of you,' he said, 'but my mother is still at the hospital and will, I know, wish to stay there as long as she is allowed. I think my father will be coming home tomorrow.'

'That's good,' Ben said.

Laura remembered what Harry had said about the police. She asked Tom if contacting them had been suggested.

'Yes, the doctor mentioned it to my father but he got very distressed. He was adamant that he did not want the police involved. He said once he knew what had happened, then he would consider it, but not till then. So that was how the matter was left.'

Tom left soon afterwards and the rest

of the day passed quickly and without incident.

Tuesday morning, too, was busy with the arrival of Lieutenant Patterson and his men to take over the crypt. The chapel was only a five-minute walk away from the manse and Ben was like an eager child wanting to go round there and watch them move in. He came back for his mid-day meal eager to relate to Laura what was taking place.

'They had the whole place neat as a new pin in next to no time,' he announced. 'Then the camp beds were put up and it's home from home down there now. When the children came out of school at dinner time there was a real crowd gathered. The lads are very friendly and the children were quite excited.'

Not just the children, Laura thought with a smile.

In the early afternoon, Harry turned up. Laura's heart leaped at the sight of him, but not with apprehension or uncertainty, only with love and eagerness to be near him.

'Why aren't you in school, Harry?' she asked him as she let him in.

'Not playing truant, my dear, just a free lesson.'

He kissed her hurriedly before they went through into the living-room where Ben was removing his slippers and putting on his shoes preparatory to going for a little stroll, which meant, of course, he was heading for the crypt again!

'I'm glad you're here, Ben,' Harry said. 'It's you I want to see.'

'Oh, well, I know when I'm not wanted,' Laura said.

Harry laughed and Ben said, 'Well, I was going to be busy this afternoon, Harry,' which was most unlike him as he was always the first to offer help.

'Now, Dad,' Laura scolded him, 'listen to what Harry has to say. Perhaps it's important.'

Ben looked chastened as he replied, 'Yes, of course. Sorry, Harry.'

Harry sat down.

'Peter's come home and he's asking for you, Ben. He won't talk to anybody else.'

'But wouldn't he be better talking to a Catholic priest? Father Stefan for instance. I'm sure he would be only too happy . . .'

Harry broke in.

'No, I suggested that to him but Father Stefan won't do. It isn't a question of making a formal confession, Ben. At least I don't think it is.'

'I hope not, because if it is I am hardly qualified.'

'Please come and see him for yourself,' Harry suggested. 'If you're uncomfortable, you'll just have to say so, but won't you at least see him?'

Ben got up.

'Of course I'll see him. Now, do you think?'

'As soon as you can. He's in a bad state, Ben. Physically on the mend, but, well, you'll no doubt learn for yourself.'

Harry didn't accompany Ben to the

138

big house, saying quite honestly that he needed to spend time with Laura, which was fine with her! But when they were alone, at first, all thcy seemed able to talk about was Peter and the alarming change in him since having his accident, if indeed that's what it had been. Laura asked if Harry had any idea what was troubling Peter so much.

'I'm not sure,' he said. 'It's obvious that for some reason he mistrusts Tom, but as to why that should be . . . '

He shrugged his shoulders helplessly.

'And Anton? Laura asked. 'Any news of him?'

'Not a word.'

'Is it possible . . . could it be, do you think . . . well, do you think Anton is involved in some way with what happened to Peter?'

Harry didn't answer and Laura could see by his expression that this thought had already occurred to him.

'You do, don't you?' she pressed him.

'We have no proof of that, Laura,' Harry said eventually.

'He's missing, isn't that proof enough?'

'Not really. Tom told us his cousin is noted for his disappearing acts.'

But Laura was not convinced. Once the idea had entered her head it was difficult to dislodge. She remembered that Anton had made her feel slightly uncomfortable. Of course, that didn't mean he was the attacker and, really, she argued with herself, why should he be? Peter Bronowski was his uncle, Anya was his late mother's sister.

'Let's wait till Ben has spoken to Peter,' Harry suggested.

He put his arms round her and drew her close.

'No suspicions of me today, Laura?'

'Oh, yes, I've got plenty of those,' she said with a smile.

'But whilst I'm alone with you I don't need to use my stick, I take it?'

'When will you tell me the truth, Harry?'

Laura's voice was serious.

'As soon as I can, I promise. And I

don't mean at the end of the war. It might be sooner than you think.'

'And I shall have to be content with that, I suppose.'

'You'll have to be content with that,' he agreed.

'In that case, I'll make you some tea.'

But Harry held on to her.

'No tea. We don't often get a chance to be alone and I have to get back to school before long.'

He looked deep into her eyes.

'Laura, let's get married. I don't want to wait until after the war. I can't wait so long, can you?'

Laura took a deep breath. To be Harry's wife was what she wanted more than anything in the world. To accept his proposal would be the final proof that she trusted him at last.

'I'm renting my own place,' Harry went on. 'I move in there at the weekend. Your father can marry us and we can live there together. Please, don't look at me like that. You're putting the fear of God into me.'

'Oh, Harry.'

At last Laura was able to speak.

'I will marry you, whenever you want me to.'

They sealed their betrothal with a long kiss.

'Of course,' Harry said with a smile, 'I'll have to ask your father for your hand in marriage, I suppose.'

'Naturally. We've got to do things right.'

'Is he likely to refuse, do you think?'

'Not a chance. He's been trying to get me married off for years.'

They laughed. It was a wonderful moment and when Harry eventually left to go back to school, Laura floated around on a cloud. What sort of a wedding would it be? Could she have a proper wedding dress? Would there be a cake? They wouldn't be able to forget there was a war on, she knew that, but she wanted to be a real bride with a bouquet, even if it was only a bunch of wild flowers, and at least one brides-maid. Shirley! Oh, she'd be thrilled to be a bridesmaid, Laura was sure.

When her father eventually returned from the big house, Laura ran to meet him as soon as she heard the front door opening, but she stopped abruptly at the sight of his worried expression.

'Is Peter all right?' she asked anxiously.

'Yes, he's well. Didn't even need stitches. Still suffering from a bad headache, but yes, he's all right.'

'But something's wrong, I can tell,' Laura went on. 'What is it, Dad?'

Ben hung up his coat and hat without speaking. Then, putting his arm around Laura's shoulders, he led her into the living-room.

'Peter told me a terrible story, Laura. In fact, I can hardly believe it. I need to contact Harry because, for the life of me, I don't know how to handle what I've been told. Don't worry, it isn't sacrosanct. I insisted Peter knew that from the outset, and he wants me to tell Harry before any decision is made.'

'Tell him what, Dad?'

Laura was getting agitated now. Ben sat down before answering. When he looked up at her, Laura could see his eyes held a look of infinite sadness.

'It seems that Tom is a traitor.'

7

Laura ran all the way to the school. As her feet pounded along the pavement she was thinking, it isn't true, it can't be! Not Tom, not kind, gentle Tom! Her father's words echoed in her mind.

'It seems that Tom is a traitor.'

He wouldn't tell her anything else.

'Fetch Harry,' was all he said. 'I know he might be teaching a class but he'll be able to get away. Tell him it's very important, Laura.'

Another phrase came to her — innocent until proven guilty. That's what she must latch on to. She had finally learned to trust Harry, hadn't she? She mustn't, she couldn't believe that Tom would betray his country or the country that had given his family refuge.

What had Peter told Ben? He must have proof. He wouldn't have spoken out against his only son, his beloved son, if he hadn't. Was Tom the one who had hit Peter on the head? Tom, by his own admission, had left the house, to chop wood he said, to go for a walk, after arguing with Anton. Perhaps it had been Peter, not Anton, with whom he had argued.

Inside the school building Laura headed straight for Mr Hiram's office, praying he would be there. He was sitting behind his desk and luckily he was alone when he answered Laura's knock and asked her to go in. He stood up when he saw who his visitor was. She was panting heavily.

'Miss March! Laura!' he cried. 'Is something wrong?'

'I've come to get Harry,' she gasped. 'My father's sent me to get Harry. Please, may I go to him? I can't tell you why, I'm sorry.'

Geoffrey Hiram wasn't about to start asking questions when he could see this young woman was plainly distressed.

'Of course. Do you know where his class is?'

Laura shook her head.

'Then I'll take you. Are you all right, Laura? Can I help in any way?'

'No, I just need Harry. Please!'

Mr Hiram said no more. At the door to Harry's classroom he stopped.

'I'll go and get somebody to take Harry's class,' he said.

The classroom door and inner wall was half-partitioned in glass. Harry looked up when he heard them approaching and seeing Laura, he strode over to the door to open it for her.

'Laura!' he cried.

'Harry, come to the house with me, please. Dad's come back from the big house. He wants to talk to you, urgently. Mr Hiram knows. He's sending someone to take your class.'

Harry addressed the goggle-eyed children.

'I'm leaving you for a while. There'll be another teacher along in a minute. In the meantime I want you all to open your reading books at page twenty-seven and start reading, quietly, to yourselves. Any noise and you'll answer to me for it.'

With this grim warning, the boys and girls quickly found their books of poems and bent over them, flicking through the pages. Laura took a quick glance around the room, thankful that Shirley wasn't in Harry's class that day. The less that young lady knew the better!

They hardly spoke as they walked back to the manse, apart from Harry saying, 'Take it easy, Laura. You've obviously run all the way here.'

He didn't ask her one single question but his face was serious, as though he had an idea what sort of news he was about to hear.

Ben was waiting for them, pacing anxiously up and down.

'Harry,' Ben said, 'thanks for coming.'

Harry sat down and Ben followed him. Laura took a chair opposite her father. Her mouth was dry and she was still trying to catch her breath. She wondered if she should make some tea, but thought better of it. They wouldn't want it, she was sure.

'Come on, Ben,' Harry urged. 'Tell me everything.'

Ben began.

'This is Peter's story, not mine, remember. I'll try to tell it in exactly the same way he told me. After we left on Saturday night, the two young men started arguing. Tom was berating his cousin for acting so boorishly. Anton called Tom a sanctimonious bore. The situation quickly became very heated, with both Tom and Anton flinging insults at one another.

'Anya tried to intervene but it didn't do any good. Then Peter stepped in, taking charge, making it plain he was having none of that sort of behaviour under his roof. Anya started crying and said she was going to bed, and Peter told her that was probably the best place to be. He kissed her good-night and she went upstairs. Then it became a question of a three-sided argument and Peter admits he lost his temper.

'At that point, Anton stormed out of the house and after further words between Peter and his son, Tom also went out, but before he did he insisted on shaking hands with Peter. They even embraced. However, once alone, Peter found he was nervy and on edge. His desire for sleep had left him and he felt he must find something to do.

'Then he remembered Anya telling him of the loose floorboards in Tom's room. She had been on at him for days to do something about them, complaining that every time she went in there they creaked and seemed to give in. Peter decided there was no time like the present. He had no worries that any hammering he might do would disturb Anya. As you know, the house is enormous and Tom's room was apparently nowhere near Peter's and Anya's. Peter went and got a claw hammer in case it was needed, perhaps to remove any nails, and went upstairs.

'He turned back the rug above the squeaking floorboards and saw what appeared to be sawn-through areas on the planks of wood. Then he kneeled down to investigate more closely.'

Ben paused and looked first at Harry then at Laura.

'Peter found that he could easily remove two of the pieces of floorboard. There was a hollow space underneath and there appeared to be something inside. It turned out to be a black box. When Peter opened it, he found it contained a radio transmitter, in fact, all the equipment to make transmissions. The implications were obvious.'

Laura broke in.

'Couldn't the radio be there for a legitimate reason, Dad? It surely didn't have to mean Tom was working for the Nazis.'

But her argument was weak and with a sick feeling in her stomach, she knew it.

'Well, Laura,' Ben went on, 'of course this occurred to Peter, too, and as he kneeled there on the bedroom floor with the box open before him he told himself he must give his son the benefit of the doubt. He must confront him, give him a chance to explain himself. He got to his feet, lifting the box as he did so. He said it was very heavy, but at that moment he was struck viciously from behind, and as he fell he must have caught the side of his head on the box.

'The two blows he had sustained knocked him unconscious. The rest of the story you know, except for the fact that when Peter got back from the hospital, he went to see if the box was still there. Naturally, it was not. Peter drew his own conclusions. And, though it saddens me, I think we must do the same.'

'What to do now is the burning question,' Harry said.

'Shouldn't we go to the authorities, tell them what we know?' Ben asked.

'Is that what Peter wants you to do?'

'Well, yes . . . I mean, obviously he doesn't want to denounce his own son, but we can't just do nothing,

Harry. You must see that.'

'Of course,' Harry said quietly, 'but I want you to leave this with me, Ben, just for the time being. I'd like to confront Tom about what we know, see what he has to say.'

'But whatever he knows, won't he deny all knowledge of it?'

'Not necessarily, Ben, and then, there's Anton.'

'Oh, come on now, you can't believe they're both involved!'

Harry stood up.

'Bear with me, Ben,' he said. 'A day or two, that's all I'm asking.'

Ben got up, too. He spoke angrily which was most unusual.

'And in the meantime Tom could be using that transmitter to contact the enemy. God alone knows what damage he's done already.'

But Harry was adamant and in the end Ben gave in, allowing Harry to swear him to secrecy for the time being. Laura, whilst balking at the knowledge that Tom was an enemy agent, still found Harry's attitude worrying and a small niggle of doubt crept into her mind. She said nothing, except to give her own promise of silence.

It wasn't until Harry had left that she remembered they had agreed to get married and that they hadn't told her father yet but, suddenly, it didn't seem so important or exciting any longer.

Laura and her father were like two caged lions for the rest of the day, restless, edgy, unable to settle to anything. On the other hand, neither seemed able or willing to talk about the implications of Peter's discovery. It hung in the air like a cloud of doom. Laura was glad when Shirley came home from school, to be able to hear her cheerful chatter.

That evening was Girl Guide night and Shirley would be going out. The meetings were held in the chapel and Shirley insisted on going alone. She wasn't scared of the dark, she said, and she usually met up with some of her friends on the way. That night, however, there was no vestige of light, it being a moonless night with thick, low clouds, and Laura stood anxiously in the doorway watching Shirley walking down the path.

'Take my torch, Shirley,' she called out.

'Don't need it!' Shirley called back cheerfully then she gave a wave and went on her way.

She would be gone for about an hour. The house seemed quiet without her. Ben went to his study soon after Shirley left. It seemed as though he needed to be alone. Usually on the evenings he was home he would sit and read or listen to the wireless. He wouldn't be writing his sermon till later in the week, so what was he doing shut away like that? What was he thinking?

Laura put on the wireless herself but when she heard Victor Sylvester's unmistakable music drifting out she turned it off again. She wished Harry would call, but knew he wouldn't. She didn't expect to see him again until he had come to a decision as to what they should do. It was odd, in a way, that she and her father followed his lead, as though he was a person in authority who knew exactly what he was doing. There was some sort of comfort knowing that Harry had been told all that had happened, a shifting of the burden from Ben's shoulders anyway, Laura thought.

Later, she made some cocoa and took a mug to her father with a couple of biscuits. She found him sitting at his desk doing nothing. The room was chilly. The fire had burned very low.

'Come back in the other room, Dad,' Laura urged him, touching his hand where it lay on the desk. 'You're icy cold.'

'I'm all right,' he said. 'Thanks for the cocoa.'

Laura put her arm round him and kissed the top of his head.

'Try not to worry, Dad. You trust Harry, don't you?'

'Yes, I do. There has never been any

question of my not trusting Harry.'

That's more than could be said for me, Laura thought.

Ben glanced at the old clock ticking slowly on the mantelpiece.

'Shirley's late, isn't she?' he remarked.

Yes, she was. Laura hadn't realised it.

'Should I go look for her, do you think?' she said.

'I shouldn't. She won't thank you for it.'

But when another half hour went by and Shirley still hadn't come home, Laura began to get really anxious. By that time Ben had moved back into the living-room, glad to reach his hands out to the cheery blaze of the log fire.

'I'm going out, Dad,' Laura said. 'Something's wrong.'

Her father tried to make light of the situation.

'What could possibly be wrong, darling? The chapel's such a short distance away.'

'That's what makes it worse. Shirley should have been home ages ago.'

Laura went to get her coat but before she could put it on someone knocked on the door. She put out the hall light as she opened the door. In the darkness she saw two figures. One was Shirley, whose head was bent forward and the other was a young man dressed in army uniform, who had his arm around Shirley's bent shoulders. Laura ushered them both inside. With the door shut and the light on again she gasped when she saw the gash on Shirley's forehead.

'Don't worry, miss, it looks worse than it is,' the young soldier assured her, in a pronounced Scottish burr.

'What happened?'

They went into the living-room. Ben leaped to his feet. Shirley was groaning and seemed disorientated.

'I found this young lady wandering around the village. Apparently in the darkness she'd walked into a wall and banged her head. She was a wee bit confused, so I took her back to the crypt with me and tended the wound on her head. She's been awful lucky, it isn't deep. My sergeant says he doesn't think she needs to see a doctor, though of course, miss, that's up to you.'

Shirley was sitting in Ben's chair by then and was looking a little better.

'I'm very grateful,' Laura began, 'for your bringing Shirley home. What's your name?'

'I'm Private Mackay.'

He had a pleasant face and a lot of freckles. He had removed his cap and revealed he also had a shock of red hair. He seemed very young, and could be no more than eighteen or nineteen.

'Can we get you a cup of tea, Private Mackay?' Ben asked.

'No, thank you. I'd better be getting back.'

He went and bent down to speak to Shirley.

'Now, young woman, no more walking into walls. That's kind of silly, wouldn't you say?'

Shirley managed a small smile.

'I should have taken a torch after all, Laura,' she said.

'Never mind,' Laura said. 'So long as you're all right. Say thank you to Private Mackay for bringing you home.'

Shyly, Shirley thanked him.

'Think nothing of it,' he said. 'Any time.'

When Laura had seen the private out she returned to the living-room. Ben was sitting on the arm of Shirley's chair, his hand on her shoulder.

'Well, Laura,' he said with a smile, 'I thought things couldn't get any worse, but it's true what they say around here, it never rains but it pours!'

Despite the gravity of the situation they were still in, Laura felt a sudden lifting of her spirits.

'There's another saying, too, Dad,' she said. 'Never say die.'

8

It was Thursday before Harry contacted them again. By then, both Laura and Ben were beginning to feel the strain of waiting. Luckily, whenever Shirley was in the house, she seemed to talk non-stop mainly about the young soldier who had come to her rescue that pitch black night. He was her knight in shining armour and Laura had a sneaking suspicion that Shirley detoured past the chapel on her way to and from school just on the off chance that she might catch a glimpse of him.

Harry didn't come personally to the manse, but sent one of the oldest boys to deliver a message for him.

'Mr Lomax says can you and Mr March meet him at the big house tonight at half-past-seven, miss?'

'Yes, we'll be here,' Laura said.

She and her father walked in silence

up to the big house. Shirley had gone to a friend's house for tea and they would call for her on their way home. It was Peter who answered the door to them.

'Good evening, Ben, Laura,' he greeted. 'Please, come in.'

Once more, a cheery fire burned in the drawing-room grate. Peter took their coats and hats, urging them to sit down. Laura noticed that he was looking pale and tense. He still had a piece of sticking plaster on his temple.

'My Anya is not here,' Peter told them as he sat down as well. 'She sends her apologies, of course, but she has gone to spend the evening with some Polish friends in town, part of a small Polish community introduced to us by Father Stefan. You remember Father Stefan?'

'Indeed we do,' Ben answered.

Peter went on, 'Anya didn't want to go but I persuaded her because Harry had said it would be best if she wasn't here. I tried to get him to tell me why but he said to wait as he would tell me everything tonight.'

'And Tom? Where is he?' Ben asked.

'On Wednesdays Tom stays late in Leeds. Hc attends a meeting of the students' union. Harry deliberately chose tonight because of that reason.'

'Still no news of Anton?' Ben went on.

'Not a word.'

Laura wished Harry would come. He was already nearly ten minutes late. What would he have to tell them? What had he been doing since Tuesday? All sorts of questions were scurrying through Laura's mind and she was sure the same questions would be plaguing her father. When the doorbell sounded, piercing the air, Laura jumped, then sat with clenched fists waiting for Peter to answer the ring.

He came back with Harry, who had already removed his coat and hat. He greeted Laura and Ben, but his face was unsmiling. Laura's heart went out to him. Poor Harry, the bearer of bad news, she was sure, but even in such a tense moment she could not stop the love for this man flowing over her.

'There is one other to come,' he stated as he sat down.

'Who?' Peter asked, puzzled. 'Have you located Anton?'

Harry looked at him.

'No, not Anton. It's Tom.'

Peter leaped up.

'Tom? Are you mad? This meeting is because of Tom, is it not? He was supposed to be in Leeds, out of the way. This is driving me insane. I do not know how much more of it I can take.'

'Don't upset yourself, Peter. You have nothing to fear from Tom.'

As he spoke those words, the drawing-room door opened and Tom walked in. Without a word he moved immediately towards the fire to warm himself. Then he went and sat on the couch beside his father.

'Poppa,' he said, inclining his head.

'Let us all try to keep calm,' Harry said.

He stood up and with a rather

theatrical gesture, tossed his cane to the other side of the room.

'There, no further use for that.'

To demonstrate his meaning, he walked slowly up and down the room, with only the faint limp Laura had noticed when she saw him in Bletchfield.

'Well, I'm blowed!' Ben exclaimed.

But Peter reacted angrily.

'So you aren't a cripple. You pretended you were. I suppose you must have your reasons, Harry, but what have they to do with the transmitter in Tom's room, or the fact that he hit me over the head?'

'I did not hit you, Poppa,' Tom said.

'Then who did?' Peter flared at him.

'That's where I come in,' Harry said. 'Don't misunderstand me. I wasn't your assailant, but I know who was, and I know why, and if you'll all bear with me I'll tell you, but it isn't going to be easy to take. Tom already knows part of what I'm about to tell you. That's how much I trust your son, Peter.'

You could have cut the air with a knife.

'We are waiting, Harry,' Peter intoned.

Harry sat down. Without pretending to be lame, he was able to sit comfortably back in the deep armchair.

'First, my bogus disability,' he began. 'In actual fact, I did have a leg injury but not through a car accident. I was shot in the leg whilst I was in Vienna on Government business. The wound healed very well and left me with only a slight limp, but when I needed an alias, shall we say, it seemed feasible to pretend to be worse than I was, to explain my non-participation in active military duty. I did train as a teacher. As Ben and Laura are well aware, I was here previously, teaching at Winford council school. It was then that I fell in love with your daughter, Ben, a love that has never died.'

Laura blushed, but Harry went on.

'Unfortunately, I was called away, a situation I couldn't avoid. I expected to be returning, but circumstances, not the least being the unrest throughout Europe, prevented me. Then, in Vienna, as I've already said, I was shot. There's no need for me to go into great detail about that. Suffice to say that I spent some time in hospital. After that, I found that events that were shaping the world were also overtaking my own life. Returning to Winford was impossible and I had no way of knowing when it would be possible so, of course, I could not even think of coming back to Laura.'

He smiled at her and she smiled back. Words were not necessary. She knew Harry would understand that she was thanking him, for telling her the truth, at last, though she was surprised, shocked even, by his story as indeed Ben must also be. Harry working for the Government!

Peter took the opportunity to say, 'This is all very well, Harry. All very noble and sad in a way for you and Laura, but what has it got to do with what I discovered under the floorboards in Tom's room and my subsequent vicious knock on the head?'

'I'm coming to that,' Harry said. 'I came back here some weeks ago ostensibly to accompany the evacuees who were to be billeted here in Winford. By a prior arrangement with Geoffrey Hiram, who, incidentally, was never told the truth, I was able to take up my former post as English master at the school. But my real reason for coming here was something much more sinister.'

He held out his hand to Laura who, after a second's hesitation, took hold of it and felt the warm, reassuring squeeze of Harry's fingers.

'I had hoped Laura would still be here because I was still very much in love with her. It hurt me to have to lie to her and deceive her but I didn't have any choice,' he went on.

Peter broke in, sounding agitated.

'Once again you are talking about yourself and Laura, Harry,' he warned.

'Sorry. Sorry. Now comes the difficult part. To make things easier to describe, I will tell it like a story. It's about a young man who was born out of wedlock to a respectable, well-educated woman. She never told her father who the father of her child was, and neither did she tell the boy, so he grew up very much aware that his father had abandoned him. Some years ago, this woman, his mother, died and, unknown to the rest of her family, she left a letter for her son in which she named his father and also gave details as to how he could be contacted. What he found at first came as a great shock to him. The man was married into a good family. He was wealthy and most important of all, he was a high-ranking officer in the German army.'

Harry paused, as though waiting for somebody to say something but nobody did. So he continued.

'The German officer welcomed his son and was not ashamed to present him to his family. It turned out the man had not abandoned the child in the way it had seemed, but had himself been abandoned when the boy's mother with whom he had had an affair found out she was pregnant.

'The young man was then greatly influenced, not only by his father's charismatic character, but by his way of life and his beliefs. It would not be an exaggeration to say he was brainwashed to some extent. Whatever, he embraced the Nazi cause. He wanted to help and he was persuaded to become an infiltrator. He went back to his other family and continued his normal life, with one difference. He now worked for one master, Adolf Hitler.

'When his family, under threat of persecution, came to England, the young man at first didn't accompany them, but once again he was persuaded, against his will, I may add, that he could serve Germany better by being here in England.'

Peter let out a long, low moan, burying his face in his hands, but it was

Tom who spoke in a harsh voice.

'You are talking about Anton, are you not?'

'Yes. Anton, your cousin, is the real reason I was sent to Winford in the first place.'

Laura was horrified. Anton had seemed strange to her, that was true, but how could such a quiet, reserved person be the man Harry had just described?

'And, of course, Anton was the one who had hidden the radio under the floorboards and attacked Peter when he was discovered,' Ben deduced.

'That's right,' Harry said.

Peter was sobbing quietly now.

'My poor Anya. How can I tell her? It will break her heart. Eva's boy! In some ways, he was like our own son, especially after Eva died. How could we ever have known?'

'You couldn't,' Harry told him, 'and you mustn't blame yourself, for none of it is your fault.'

Tom spoke next with an edge of

bitterness in his voice.

'So, Harry, you knew it was Anton all along. You had him under surveillance, wouldn't you say? You played out your game with scant thought for the way I was being marked as the chief suspect.'

Harry's usual even temper soared at Tom's words.

'So you think it's a game, do you, Tom? People are being betrayed and sent to camps and dying! It is not a game.'

Tom looked chastened.

'No, no, I don't think that. I apologise. You had a job to do and you did it and I am grateful for that.'

Peter took out a handkerchief and wiped his eyes.

'And what of Anton now?' he asked sadly.

'He is being watched most carefully and he will betray himself before he is through, but rest assured, he will not be allowed to betray anybody else.'

'In some ways,' Peter said, 'I am sorry for my nephew. He was swept along. He must have been flattered, overcome by a surge of loyalty to his German father. He must have then thought of himself as a true German.'

Laura was inclined to agree. What next, she wondered.

Ben stood up and walked towards Peter's chair.

'If there's anything I can do to help, Peter,' he said, 'anything at all.'

'Thank you,' Peter said, 'but if I need spiritual guidance, Father Stefan will be there for me and Anya.'

'Of course,' Ben agreed then watched as Peter stood and held out his arms to Tom.

Without a word, and after only the slightest hesitation, Tom went to his father and they embraced.

It was time to go home. There was nothing more to be said and there was a great deal to think about. Laura had to get used to the idea of the man she loved being a Government agent. The three of them, she, Harry and Ben walked slowly down the hill towards the manse, each with their own thoughts. Outside the gate, Ben suddenly spoke.

'We're forgetting about Shirley. We're supposed to be picking her up from her friend Molly's house,' he explained to Harry.

'I'll walk Laura round there,' Harry offered, 'but first I'd like to come inside for a few moments, Ben. I have something I'd like to say to you.'

He gave Laura a wink. She knew what that something was. Ben smiled.

'More secrets to reveal, young man?' he asked.

'Not really. At any rate, something much more pleasant than what's just taken place.'

They went inside. Neither Laura nor Harry removed their coats as they would be going out again shortly. Laura tended the slumbering fire, prodding it into blazing life with the poker whilst Harry faced Ben.

'I'd like, sir,' he began formally, 'to ask for your daughter's hand in marriage.'

Ben didn't look particularly surprised. He stood for a moment, looking from one to the other. Then he held out a hand to Harry and caught Harry's in both of his, pumping it vigorously.

'Of course, dear chap, I'd be delighted, provided,' he said and winked at Laura, much as Harry had done outside the gate, 'Laura agrees.'

'Oh, Dad.'

She put her arms round him and kissed his cheek.

'Yes, yes, please!'

'So when's the happy day to be?'

Ben turned to Harry again.

'As soon as possible. I'm moving into my own place this weekend and we can live there for the time being.'

'Oh, dear, I don't know if I like the sound of that,' Ben confessed.

Harry laughed.

'I'll be here for some time, Ben. I won't be getting my marching orders just yet. There are other situations to be dealt with,' he added seriously.

Ben took up his sober mood.

'Yes, yes, I don't doubt it. But haven't you more or less blown your cover?'

Harry grinned.

'Oh, you'd be surprised what yarns I can spin, Ben, all in the service of His Majesty's Government.'

Laura decided not to delve too deeply into that!

As they walked to Shirley's friend's house, arm in arm, Harry said, 'I'll buy you a ring on Saturday. Any good jewellers in Bletchfield?'

'Oh, yes. There's one very expensive shop. So far I've never been any nearer to it than pressing my nose up against the window.'

'Money's no object,' Harry said.

'No, seriously, there are other shops, Harry. I was only joking.'

'But I wasn't, my darling, Laura.'

And there and then, in the dark street, he put his arms around her and kissed her.

It was hard to let her mind dwell on the possibility that some time in the future, if the war lingered on, she and

Harry might be parted again. But at least, she thought happily, if it did happen, she would be Harry's wife.

They went up the path of the neat, little terrace house and Harry knocked on the door. It was opened by a slim woman who peered out anxiously.

'Hello, Mrs Foster,' Laura greeted. 'We've come to collect Shirley.'

The woman's anxiety seemed to deepen.

'Happen you'd better come inside, Miss March,' she said.

Laura and Harry entered the tiny living-room. An old-fashioned and decrepit-looking gas fire with missing elements gave out a cold blue warmth. Laura saw Molly sitting on the sagging couch, wearing her nightclothes, sipping from a mug of what looked like cocoa. She was the only other person in the room.

'Where's Shirley?' Laura asked sharply.

'Shirley left after she'd had her tea. Said you was expecting her home. I said to her you'd made it plain to me she was picking you up later on, but Shirley wasn't having none of that and said she was to go straight home.'

Mrs Foster shrugged her thin shoulders.

'So what was I supposed to do? Keep her here against her will?'

Laura looked at Harry. Shirley obviously hadn't gone straight home and now it was almost nine o'clock. Where on earth could she be?

A search around the virtually empty streets of the village proved fruitless. By then, Laura was nearly frantic with worry. In the end they decided to go back to the manse. Perhaps Shirley might be home. In any event, Ben would be wondering what was taking them so long.

'I hope she's got a good explanation,' Laura said grimly.

'It isn't like Shirley to be deceitful. You haven't found her so, have you?'

'Never.'

As they walked back, Harry said, 'I

hope the Bronowskis will be all right. I felt so helpless, not being able to do anything to ease Peter's pain.'

'He's a strong man,' Laura said.

'In one way I shall be glad when Anton can be picked up. When things come to a head, perhaps Peter and Anya, and Tom, too, of course, might be able to come to terms with what's happened.'

'I hope so,' Laura said fervently.

Ben was waiting anxiously and his agitation increased when Laura told him what had happened.

'You don't think . . . no, no, I'm barking up the wrong tree,' he said.

'What is it, Dad?' Laura prompted.

'Well, could she be with that young private?' Ben asked hesitatingly.

'Private Mackay?'

'Who is he?' Harry asked.

They told him. Harry looked disbelieving.

'Is that likely?' he wanted to know.

'Shirley's got quite a crush on the lad,' Ben said with a smile.

'Even so, he's an enlisted man. He wouldn't do anything foolish, would he?' Laura commented.

The three of them pondered this. Then they head the sound of the front door opening and footsteps and voices in the hall.

'Now you're for it, Miss Dobson,' Laura muttered.

Harry turned to Ben.

'I think I'll be off. If sparks are going to fly I'd rather not be here.'

'I don't blame you,' Ben said.

Harry crossed paths with Laura, Shirley and the private, the latter twisting his cap round and round nervously, as they came through into the living-room. Harry then beat a hasty retreat, whispering to Laura, 'See you tomorrow.'

Shirley's face was flushed.

'I'm sorry, honest I am, Laura. I didn't mean no harm by it.'

'But where have you been?'

Laura glared from one to the other of them.

Private Mackay spoke first.

'We've been to the flicks, Miss March, in Bletchfield.'

Laura knew where the nearest cinema was, she didn't need to be told. What she did want to hear was what they thought they were playing at. He hurried on.

'I asked Shirley if she'd like to go see a film. I said to be sure she asked permission first and she told me she had and that it was all right.'

'Oh, she did, did she?'

Laura turned to Shirley. Shirley blushed deeper than ever.

'I didn't fink you'd let me go,' she muttered.

Ben spoke for the first time.

'And you'd have been right, young woman. Private Mackay, have you any idea how old Shirley is?'

'She's sixteen.'

He looked stricken when he realised that wasn't true.

'She isn't sixteen, is she, sir?'

'She's fourteen,' Ben told him.

'Oh, blimey!' the young soldier moaned.

'Blimey indeed,' Ben agreed.

'You must have realised she was still at school,' Laura remarked.

'Well, yes, well, I didn't think at all, really, did I? I'm so sorry, miss.'

It was to his credit that despite his obvious misery and remorse he didn't try to blame Shirley.

'Well, I don't suppose there's any real harm done.'

Ben looked hopefully at Laura as he spoke.

'Oh, no, sir, it was all above board and I had a pass, sir. Would you like to see it?'

'No, I'll take your word for that.'

'Thank you, sir. Thank you, miss.'

The young soldier's relief was plain to see. At the door on his way out he spoke to Shirley.

'Thank you for a wonderful evening, Shirley,' and then he was off as fast as his legs would carry him.

Laura had visions of him running like

mad all the way to his billet.

'I'm ever so sorry, Laura,' Shirley said.

'Yes, so you keep saying.'

'I won't do it again, cross my heart and hope to die.'

'I should think not, indeed,' Ben cried. 'Now off to bed with you before I take my slipper to you!'

But he was smiling now, relieved that all had ended well. Laura smiled, too. Grinning, Shirley skipped out of the room.

Ben and Laura sat down at last, on either side of the fire, hoping the rest of the evening would pass uneventfully.

'She's growing up fast,' Ben said dreamily. 'I well remember a certain Miss Laura March at fourteen years of age.'

Laura pretended to be offended.

'I was a very well-behaved, young lady.'

'Yes, you were,' her father agreed. 'But never a goody-two-shoes.'

'Would you have wanted me to be?'

'No, I don't suppose I would,' Ben said with a sigh.

He changed the subject.

'So you and Harry are to be married. I'm glad you've decided not to wait until the war is over. Life is too short. Are you nervous at all, darling, about marrying a man in Harry's profession? And I'm not talking about him being a schoolmaster.'

'A little,' Laura admitted, 'but I love him, Dad, with all my heart and I want us to be together.'

'Good, good. And you're not to worry about me, do you hear? I've been thinking, I might get a full-time housekeeper when you're married. I can't really have Shirley living here with me on my own.'

To Laura's shame this was something that had not occurred to her, though no doubt it would have, given time.

'You'd do that, Dad?' she asked.

'Willingly. Shirley's happy here and I'm happy to have her, for as long as she needs a home and someone to love her in place of her mother.'

Remembering how he had brought her up with love, affection and under-standing and only a sprinkling of gentle discipline, Laura knew how well Ben March would do the job of surrogate parent. She went to him, put her arms around him and kissed him.

'Thanks, Dad,' she said.

She didn't go back to her chair, but continued to sit on the arm of Ben's. This was a close and tender moment after the upheaval of the day. For the Bronowskis, Laura knew, the turmoil, the anguish was only just beginning, but she hoped they would find it possible to remain in Winford for as long as they wanted to. They had friends here, people who would sympa-thise and understand what they were going through.

Laura wanted to invite them to her wedding. It wouldn't be just yet. There were things to arrange, but, as with the bonfire party, she wanted her marriage to Harry to be a village affair, for all toenjoy and remember in the years to come.

And there would be good years ahead — she was sure of it.

THE END